DOCTOR TUCK

DOCTOR TUCK

Elizabeth Seifert

Thorndike Press • Chivers Press
Thorndike, Maine USA Bath, England

This Large Print edition is published by Thorndike Press, USA and by Chivers Press, England.

Published in 1998 in the U.S. by arrangement with Blassingame-Spectrum Corporation.

Published in 1998 in the U.K. by arrangement with Ralph Vicinaza Limited.

U.S. Hardcover 0-7862-1538-0 (Candlelight Series Edition)
U.K. Hardcover 0-7540-3455-0 (Chivers Large Print)
U.K. Softcover 0-7540-3456-9 (Camden Large Print)

Copyright © 1977 by Elizabeth Seifert

All rights reserved.

The text of this Large Print edition is unabridged.
Other aspects of the book may vary from the original edition.

Set in 16 pt. Plantin by Minnie B. Raven.

Printed in the United States on permanent paper.

British Library Cataloguing in Publication Data available

Library of Congress Cataloging in Publication Data

Seifert, Elizabeth, 1897–
　　Doctor Tuck / by Elizabeth Seifert.
　　　　p.　cm.
　　ISBN 0-7862-1538-0 (lg. print : hc : alk. paper)
　　1. Physicians — Middle West — Family relationships
— Fiction.　I. Title.
　[PS3537.E352D578　1998]
　　813'.52—dc21　　　　　　　　　　　　　　98-25151

DOCTOR TUCK

One

Tuck groaned. Hearing the noise he made echo and rebound from the walls of the bathroom, the big man laughed at his face in the mirror, and then he groaned again.

"I am absolutely going to find me a job," he told his mirrored face, "where, if I want — at six in the morning — I can roll over and go back to sleep. You can't do that in the profession I am in." He leaned forward, examining the job he had done with the razor, and grinned. Nobody but Carrie cared if he had a smooth shave.

But Carrie was enough. Carrie was everything.

Whistling now, he finished dressing, pulled a turtleneck over his head, checked to see if he had left the bathroom tidy. "The worst part of being a bachelor," he sometimes informed his friends, "is that you have to put things away. Otherwise, you have to do it yourself later. So a guy might as well —"

He picked up a leather jacket, which he slung over his shoulder. He would not need it in the car. And he went out of the house. He called it his cabin.

Carrie said that no house, A-frame or whatever, could be called a cabin if it had a big, broad mirror over the fireplace. A stone fireplace, with a hand-hewn, hand-rubbed oak mantel.

"Cabin," muttered Tuck, stepping out on the frosty, crackly grass.

He looked up at the sky. In the eastern heavens there were gold and red-rimmed purple clouds; the rising sun showed as a brilliant red streak along the horizon; the spruce trees and the pines and birches were dark against that sky. The air was misty; it always was close to the lake. His lake. This whole area was more lake than land, big ones, little ones, and Tuck's lake, which that morning was like a pewter tray, except that no tray would tremble under the light wind, no tray would invite the water birds. Ducks, a crane over in the rushes, and a gaggle of geese talking to each other. He liked that word, and he repeated it to himself as he started the car, backed, and turned it toward the city. "Gaggle . . ." The conversation of the geese sounded as if they had used the word.

He must tell Carrie about that when he saw her — he glanced at his watch — in twenty-nine minutes, and she would call him a nut, but her smile would be loving. *"Yoweeee!"* he said softly, shifting his back in the car seat, turning the car's wheels into the main road.

"Look out for the runners," he told himself. He had a habit of talking half-aloud, not always alone when he did it. In the cabin, it didn't matter. But he had caught a smile or two in o.r. Though, to date, only Carrie had mentioned it to him. "Why I worked up to Chief," he said. "Can do as I please."

Sometimes.

And here came the expected runners. Along the foot-paths by the lake, on the grass of the median and shoulders, weaving through traffic, up and down the bridges. Tuck knew them all. Some of them knew him, called out to him, or waved. Here came a big, bearded man in a T-shirt and shorts. Flab jiggling all over his body. A white-haired couple chugged briskly up a small hill. A skinny, shirtless man with a fuzzy beard and a painter's hat zipped past Tuck's car. Three young women in sweat shirts plodded steadily along. Two men in old track jerseys loped with long, easy strides. Tuck leaned forward and slowed the car. Over there by the intersection was a fellow leaning into the bushes in some discomfort. Tuck dropped the window.

"Can I help, sir?" he called. "Give you a lift?"

The man turned his unhappy face. "Hangover," he gasped.

Tuck laughed. "Get in. I'm a doctor."

The fellow shook his head. "I think — I'll lie down —" he gasped. "And die."

Tuck laughed again, and drove off. The fellow would recover. And most likely never jog or run again.

Now he had come to another lake, and smiled broadly. For now the lake water and the whole sky was pink, and the little wavelets were beginning to sparkle and shine. Oh, gee, pops! He wished he could just stay out of doors and enjoy! This thing of sterile, sealed-against-fresh-air operating rooms was bad! How had he ever committed himself to such a life?

Why shouldn't he be just Tucker Fairbairn sitting out on the brick stoop of his cabin, enjoying his own lake, and listening to the geese gaggle?

He squared his shoulders. Traffic was getting a bit wild here close to the city, the towers of which were rising before him, purple-gray against the haze. Square towers, a round one, a peaked top to a skinny one. The flash of sunlight upon one building that was all glass and steel. And a whole cluster, a whole *gaggle*, of buildings that was his own complex, his own hospital, his own prison on such a beautiful autumn morning. Of course his particular building did not do much sticking up, here or otherwise. It was only six stories high, spread out extravagantly, with the patients' windows each having a view, the doctors, offices and o.r.'s and stuff without even *windows*. But it was a fine, new building, and should be appreciated. In its first year some waggish intern or student had labeled it SKULL AND BONES. Because Neurology occupied the three top floors, and the orthopeds took over the lower ones. Some of the staff deplored the name. Tuck thought they should put it on the building's wall and take down all the pompous letters that spelled institute and neurological research, orthopedic procedure . . . stuffy names like that! Skull and Bones it was, indeed!

He had never discussed the matter with an older patient, but the kids loved it. Shocked their mothers, but they loved it. He had more kids than adults, poor little boogers. Some diseases were a rough go for them. So Skull and Bones it was.

He had to wait on the light — as always. The complex was approached, and entered, by way of a wide esplanade, or circle, complete with bronze light standards, a flower bed, even a bright-shafted fountain. The street surface was painted with directions, to parking areas, to the through street. And stern warnings. STAY IN LANE. YIELD. KEEP TO THE RIGHT. Things like that. Sometimes, coming to the hospital in the small hours because of an emergency, Tuck had dared to cross lanes. But not at this hour of the morning, with doctors and nurses and all sorts of people reporting in, apprehensive families, and — oh, gee, pops! — even an ambulance. Roaring down the wide boulevard, waking everybody in the posh apartments, even in the hotel three blocks away, bringing the bus waiters-for to the curb to peer after it. Lights flashing, siren and howler going. *A-whoopa, a-whoopa, screeech!*

Tuck sat with his hand on the wheel, and waited, his rugged face impassive, though inwardly he was smiling at himself. An M.D. for nearly twenty years, his pulse and blood pressure could always respond to an ambulance siren. "*Sireeens,*" his grandmother had called them, and the name was good. The shrill warning signal could send an icy chill down his spine, raise prickles on the back of his neck, raise the hair on his arms, and squeeze his guts. It could also — His eye flitted to the speedometer. This was no place to accelerate!

He skillfully negotiated the driveway, and slid his car down the ramp and into its allotted place in the garage built beneath the aforesaid esplanade, circle, or whatever one chose to call the thing. A clever use of expensive space, but parking in it did not put the Meds very close to their jobs. Some of those same Meds did a bit of jogging as they went to their buildings' elevators. Tucker walked, his long legs pushing the distance behind him, his mind beginning to repeat the schedule which had been spoken to him on his wake-up telephone call. Meetings, rounds, o.r. — two of 'em — post-op, rounds again with a class. This morning the siren was hurrying his step, sharpening his attention. He heard sounds distinctly which generally blurred into the continuous noise of any hospital corridor, people talking, feet slapping the concrete, the tile — a distant bell, a close-at-hand coded signal. Repeated, as always. That had to be done. The first call only alerted the person wanted. The repeat told him, or her, or *them* what was required. This morning, Tuck heard each one, his ears laid back, like the fire-horse he was.

"I should switch to emergency," he told himself. "I pump adrenalin at each bleep!"

He also greeted and answered the greetings of his colleagues, of the personnel. "Hello, Hazel!" to the orange-smocked maid with her mop. "Hi-ya, Carson!" to the brain surgeon.

Waiting for the elevator at the top of the ramp, he turned to look back at the garage, rapidly filling with cars, their shining tops lined as expertly and efficiently as the helmet tops of deployed troops.

Well . . .

". . . should switch to emergency . . ." Tuck repeated softly, swiftly thinking of a fellow doctor. A friend. Older than Tuck by fifteen years, he had given up ortho-surgery for an eight-to-five job in an emergency area of a large hospital complex in Florida. He was a prime surgeon, he cared for his patients; Tuck had known him to sit all night at the bedside of a touch-and-go case. But he claimed to like his new work. He could receive cases, decide triage, attend to some himself and send them off to the wards or home, or — well, he never saw any of them again. And he could sleep at nights, sail his boat by day . . . Or, could he?

"I'll bet he thinks of some of the banged-up ones," Tuck said softly to the hampers of linens which were filling two thirds of the elevator.

"Serves me right," he grinned, "if they'd give me an argument." They did not talk back, and Tuck emerged on his floor, still smiling. Emergency duty might be all right for the older surgeon. It would never be right for Tuck Fairbairn.

From the time he was ten years old, and ever since, he had been and was a surgeon ready to be taught, to learn, to practice, and to learn again. He liked, he wanted, to see new patients, to examine them, to talk to them, to go along with them in whatever procedure was decided upon, to know the family as completely as he studied and came to know the case, to help each patient individually, and follow up any surgery he advised or himself performed. Emergency duty was like reading the first chapter of a book, and casting it aside — Tuck —

He came out on the third floor, his floor, and went to the desk, touched the computer signal which signed him in. "Damned machine!" he growled to himself. He spoke to the charge nurse and asked — heard by all within twenty feet — "Want to hear a joke?"

He nearly always had a joke with which

to start a day. The hospital expected it of him. Good or bad, they got one each morning, and often repeated it when their duties took them elsewhere.

"This morning, Dr. Fairbairn told a good one," they would say.

This morning, good or bad, he told his joke. Glancing from one expectant face to the other, his own black eyes sparkling but his face serious.

"Did you know," he asked, "that the largest dinosaur that ever lived was a bronchitis?"

One of the nurses giggled. Tuck nodded. "It soon became extinct," he said quietly, even as he picked up a chart. "It coughed a lot."

Now everyone laughed. "Was that original, doctor?" asked the resident seated at the desk.

"Well, of course not," said Dr. Fairbairn. "What do you expect for a nickel?" He bent over the chart. "All of us comedians," he said, reaching for a second one, "steal our stuff. How's Junior this morning?" he asked the resident.

The younger doctor made a leveling gesture with his hand.

"We'll look in on him," said Tuck, "soon as I finish — these — Where's the dictionary?"

The battered red-bound book was pushed toward him. Dr. Fairbairn never pointed out a misspelled word without checking. "Dr. Moore in?" he asked, thumbing the pages.

"Yes, sir. He had a critical. He may have gone down to breakfast."

Tuck's eyebrows questioned the resident. "Yes, sir," said Dr. Tennant. Quietly.

Tuck nodded, and went through the rest of the charts. The nurse put a schedule sheet before him. "What happened to rounds?" he asked.

"I'll do them, doctor," said the resident. "Billings called in with a sore throat."

"Suppose we cut it if we ever see him again," said Dr. Fairbairn, his voice steady. "How many . . . ? Oh, gee, pops, not *three!*"

"Dr. Moore said he would do the . . ."

"Does he know the cases?"

"He's been studying the x-rays, sir."

"I am sure he has. But that's a bit different . . . Good Lord, man! Does this woman know a strange guy is going to pin her kneecap?"

Now he had a half-dozen charts spread out on the counter. His specialty was bone diseases. It kept him busy, what with overseeing the work of the other staff men. He could do surgery on an impacted elbow, he could pin a shattered kneecap, he could —

"I had other plans," he muttered, starting down the hall toward o.r. "Send Dr. Billings a pot of poison ivy with my compliments," he called over his shoulder.

Moore, his assistant, would be in o.r.; he would open and close for these three cases. He would stand shoulder to shoulder for Tuck's two.

"That elbow can take three hours!" Tuck declared, joining Moore in the viewing room.

"I suspect Billings knew that," said Dr. Moore mildly.

Tuck glanced at him and grinned. "Driving here this morning," he said, "I called myself an old firehorse."

"Not old, Tuck," said Dr. Moore obligingly.

Tuck snorted. "A few more days like this, and I'll make it," he predicted. "Is Carrie here?"

But of course she was here! She would never fail him. He stood, gazing at the x-ray plates, frowning. He glanced at Dr. Moore.

Both men knew what lay ahead for them. Tuck was to ankylose the vertebrae of a tuberculous spine, and he had an osteomyelitis which antibiotics had not cleared up.

Now, in addition, he would have the three cases which Billings had dumped. He could give a couple of these elsewhere, to other surgeons. "I want to see these people," he told Dr. Moore.

"Carrie is waiting on your decision, sir."

"She'll get it. Meanwhile we could send someone out to take a culture of Billings' throat."

It was as much of a temper as Dr. Fairbairn ever allowed himself to display. "We'll do limited rounds," he decided.

"Yes, sir." They would all be very late completing this day.

"I didn't want to come in this morning myself," he told Dr. Moore as he started for the hall. "Got your little scratch pad, doctor?"

"I do. Could I speak to Miss Reynolds?"

"Tell her there will be a thirty-minute delay."

"Yes, sir." Moore glanced at the wall phone, then decided to speak directly to the o.r. Head.

Tuck nodded, and returned to the x-rays. He knew his own by heart. He knew something of Billings', and of the patients. The middle-aged man who had a history of the infections, the thin woman of sixty who had been banged up in a car wreck. The teenager had been hurt when he'd done some drag racing with his arm hooked over the open window of his car. Elbows! He studied each x-ray intently.

And he thought about Carrie. The only good thing he could see about this stacked-up day. Should he allow her to work straight through it? If he relieved her, she would claim favoritism. Her dark blue eyes would meet his — and he would give in to her. Even in the hospital, he knew that he would always give in to Carrie. Well, he had plans for that! They were going to be married, and Carrie would stop working. It was as simple a plan as that! And he liked it. He really did.

This elbow now . . . Tuck had taken his time, of course, about marrying anybody. But at last he was ready. Right up to the wire. He would have a proper house — he could not ask Carrie to keep house in the cabin, have kids and all the rest of it there. No, they would have a house, in or near the city, a house with an upstairs, a downstairs, a basement, and an attic. And Carrie, and their family. The time had come when he would need to consider such things, to consider others before himself.

Moore returned, tall, earnest, eyeglassed. Moore put up with a lot from his Chief.

"All set, sir," he reported. "The spine is being prepped."

"Mr. Armstrong," Tuck corrected.

"Yes, sir. Miss Reynolds suggests we start with that. She's ready to bring in Shadrach to do the cast for you."

"Unless he's busy."

"She says he won't be. That will be a large cast."

"We are being managed, Moore."

"Yes, sir. But Miss Reynolds . . ."

"She makes us like it. I know."

And Tuck was going to marry that very special girl. It was worth the years he had delayed marrying. Though he had known Carrie during that time. He had known her since she was fourteen or so. Tuck had missed the marriage bit when most other men were taking care of such matters. Even men in Med school, men who had completed the school part, and certainly when they were ready to do their residencies.

Tuck could have, as well as several of them. But no, his work came first. He had to wait until he was Chief of Bone Disease Surgery in this big center. And even now — Without Carrie, he might still think his work came first. And it did. It would. But — well, he had got where he was by hard work, study, and more hard work. Now . . .

"Let's go," he said to Moore, striding out into the hall.

"You saw your own patients last night, Tuck," reminded Moore's voice at his shoulder.

"Yes, I did. But there's the delay . . ."

"Not for Armstrong."

"And Shadrach, Meshach, Abednego . . ." Tuck hummed. "Where's the kid with the elbow?" He didn't like that boy. A doctor should not feel one way or another about a patient. But of course he did.

He bent over the boy's bed. "I am Dr. Fairbairn," he said. "Dr. Billings is ill. I have been chosen to take care of the elbow you smashed."

"So?" said the lad, his hooded eyes insolent.

"So we're both stuck with each other," said Dr. Fairbairn. "And we won't get around to you at exactly the time you were told. O.K.?"

The boy shrugged, which hurt his injured arm. Tuck patted his knee. "I know how," he said, going out of the room.

Dr. Moore wrote something on his pad. He could trust Tuck.

Of course, thought Tuck, going down the hall a few steps to the next patient's room, I've never been very far for very long from this center. I was raised in this city, and I grew right along with the whole thing. Went to college, Med school, and grew big, awkward, learned what to do with my mind and my clumsy hands. The Center had things to learn, too. I watched it being built, and added to. Tuck had trained in the Center. Internships, residencies, the whole thing. Then he had gone away to Boston, to England, Sweden, and Switzerland for new training in new techniques. And returned to Skull and Bones, to its staff; two years ago he had been named Chief, Bone Diseases. He had worked hard, and well, generally. The Center had done well, generally.

He found the osteo case asleep; Dr. Fairbairn talked to the mother who sat beside the patient's bed, reading. She was white, but controlled. "Dr. Billings hoped to save his leg," she said softly.

"I am big on saving everything I can," said Dr. Fairbairn warmly. "Don't worry any more than you can help."

She managed a smile, and, departing, Tuck could find no reason not to speak to the knee lady. He had previously encountered her on rounds, and sympathized with her as the victim of a car accident not her fault. She was in pain, and worried — perhaps, in health, she was not waspish.

Though perhaps she was, for she had a husband fifteen years older than she was, who had Parkinsonism, and would not succumb to his frailties. In the last three days, his tottering, stoop-shouldered figure had become all too familiar in these halls.

This woman — Mrs. Wikerson — was not ready to accept a change in doctors graciously.

Dr. Moore told her that Fairbairn was Chief of Orthopedic Services. Only Tuck's bright eye kept him from mentioning the financial bargain she was getting. She had expected to go to o.r. at ten. She liked things to be done on schedule . . .

"So do I," said Dr. Fairbairn. "And as soon as we have rearranged these schedules, Billings' and mine, the nurse will tell you the new time." He smiled and nodded to the patient in the second bed. And left the room.

"I'm going to scrub," he told Moore. "When you get that damned schedule, see to it that I have ten minutes in it to look at Abednego's cast."

Dr. Moore wrote something on his pad. "Wait for me," he said to Tuck as he went past him toward the nurses' station.

Without needing to reply, Tuck went on toward surgery, signed in at the desk, and asked if Miss Reynolds was around. The nurse gazed at him blandly. "Three guesses, doctor," she said.

Tuck nodded. "I've been telling you, Langdon," he said, with a show of patience. "For twenty years, I've been telling you . . ."

"Twenty years ago you were sucking a lollipop, doctor," said the woman calmly. "She's on Three, where you are due to go to work in fifteen minutes."

"Then I'd better get on my bicycle, hadn't I?" Tuck asked.

"*Scrubbed!*" Mrs. Langdon called after him.

Tuck flapped his hand behind him as he opened Three's outer door.

And there she was. Carrie. His girl. She had the patient on the table, and was bending over him. Beautiful as the early morning, even in the awful blue cap, and the shapeless blue gown. Her face was pure enough to take the things. No one ever looked prettier than did Carrie in her o.r. get-up. He tapped on the door window. She looked up, smiled, and then pointed to the clock. He made gestures of scrubbing and started for the locker room on the double.

He quickly changed his clothes for scrub rompers, put his watch into his sock and fastened it to his leg with tape. "I am not pretty suited up," he said as he went through to the scrub basins. Moore was hanging the schedule on the wall, and read it aloud to Tuck. "I'll change . . ." he announced superfluously.

"You'd better," said Tuck, searching for the brush.

He knew when Carrie came in. He nearly always knew when she was close by. Now she came to him and hugged him around the waist.

"You look darling," she told him, and he chuckled.

"You *are* darling," he told her, scrubbing away. For both of them excitement lay like the shimmer of bright silk between them.

Scrub, scrub . . . splash, splash . . . their shoulders touched and drew away.

"What's the joke for the day?" Carrie asked him.

He told her, and she shook her head. "Really, Tuck!" she reproved him.

"When's the date for the wedding?" he countered.

Her eyebrows lifted, and her cheeks became a little more pink. The intern across the basin was watching them. "As soon as Bob gets better," she told Tuck.

"How is he, Carrie?" he asked.

"I go there almost every night. He plays, but sometimes he just sits. Wearily. At four, a little boy . . ." She shook her head.

"Haven't Stowe and Megan made any decision?"

Her face became still more saddened. "I've told them that delay is dangerous."

"And . . . ?"

"Stowe says he is glad I don't live with them. That he and Megan need time to think. He evidently believes that I interfere, that I pressure Megan."

"You don't interfere, do you?"

"Not beyond what I just said. I try not to . . . But both of them know how I feel."

"Because you've told them."

"A few times, yes, I have, Tuck. But as for interference, I can't keep myself from showing how strongly I feel that the boy needs help."

"Me, too," growled Tuck, stepping back from the basin. Carrie turned her head to watch him. She wished he might have kissed her, that each of them could have shown their love for the other. But by now Scrub was crowded with Tuck's surgical team.

"Too many of us," Carrie told herself.

At five minutes before eight on a busy-scheduled morning, there were too many of everything on the surgical floor. Only two of the three operating rooms would be in use, thanks to Billings' throat, but even so, stretcher carts, linen carts, shrouded machines cluttered the place. And people! All sorts of people! Most of them in scrub suits, with a few crisply uniformed nurses, even one man in a business suit. The level of talk rose, and rose. Nurses, orderlies, carts, doctors fairly swarmed. The locker rooms were worse. Noisier. Too hot, too noisy, too smelly. Men's voices hummed and lifted, jokes were told; laughter added to the row, slamming locker doors. The confusion spilled into the corridor as doors opened and closed, spilled into Scrub . . .

"A fine place for romance," thought Carrie Reynolds, finishing her own scrub, and turning, as Tuck had done, to the towels, the gown, the gloves.

When he worked, Dr. Fairbairn worked hard and steadily. Unless there was a class to be instructed, he spoke rarely and then only a word or two. From the circulating nurse to Dr. Moore and Carrie Reynolds, his surgical team had been trained and drilled to a perfection that approached his own. Scarcely ever did a hand falter, or a bobble occur. This made for security, but scarcely relaxation. Carrie sometimes described Tuck's o.r. as the casing of a fine watch. "With each little wheel and lever ticking along exactly as they should, the big wheel governing all the little ones, and its performance the best of them all."

Ankylosing a spine — seven vertebrae of that spine — fusing them exactly, particularly, caring about the nerves, the fit of each bone fragment — keenly aware of the patient who was conscious and able to plead for release, relief. "Hurry up, Doc," he said a hundred times in those three hours. And someone would answer, "He is hurrying."

Poor devil. Tuck worked steadily, he worked skillfully, the team helped — but there was time for the anaesthetist to think about the little fuss he had had with his wife that morning, for the instrument nurse to wonder if she could hope to keep the date she had for that evening, for Carrie to rearrange her plans. "I'll go past Megan's before I go home," she decided. "After five sessions in o.r., I'll be lucky if I can go downstairs," she told herself.

And Tuck did some thinking too. A lot of thinking.

Two

He thought about Bob Vashon. A child. The child of Carrie's sister Megan and her husband Stowe. Bob was four years old. He did not want to be called Bobby. He was an enchanting child, still chubby and soft-fleshed with babyhood. His hair was red-blond, cut into a thick bang above his wide, inquiring blue eyes. He talked well, he thought things out. Bob Vashon, a dandy little boy, four years old.

Bent over his patients doing his meticulous fancy work, the surgeon, Tucker Fairbairn, thought fleetingly about the first time he had met Bob. The first time he had seen the child, and that was six months ago.

"Wipe," said Carrie from across the table, and a nurse swabbed her towel across Tuck's forehead. He shook off her ministrations, but said thank you automatically.

Six months ago, yes, about that long. It was early spring, but a beautiful warm day. Tuck's day off. He had walked along the lake edge. "His" lake, which stretched quite a way into the wooded acres behind his cabin. That day the birches had trembled with new leaves, flowers were poking their pretty heads up through the leaf mold of last winter, and the winter before that.

Tuck swung his heavy cane, and looked up at the sky between the tree branches, down at the dry needles under his feet, out at the waters of the lake. They shimmered in the sunlight. The path wandered along, into the woods, down again to the water edge, out to where a point of land with a sandy beach stretched invitingly. "If I thought I really was alone . . ." Tuck murmured.

The squirrels did not matter, the chipmunks, nor any of the birds, but a time or two earlier he had thought he heard voices. And yes, he had, because coming toward him from a curve in the bank were, of all things, horses. Two horses, splashing and snorting in the shallow waters, and ridden by two girls. Young women. The dark-haired one held a child in her arms, the blond one —

"Carrie!" he shouted, turning to run toward them. They saw him and called out gaily — Carrie Reynolds, and her sister Megan, whom he had not seen in ages!

Well, at least for months. When she worked in the Records room at the Complex he had seen her regularly, in the halls, in the cafeterias — at parties of hospital people. He liked Megan; it was through her work at the Complex that he had come to know Carrie.

But, lately — Megan had married — he had gone to the wedding, actually — but it was quite a while after that when she had left the Records room on maternity leave. And this little red-headed boy . . .

"Is this what happened when you took leave?" he had asked foolishly.

He now remembered that warm, delicious afternoon there by the lake, laughter, surprise, happiness was the way he remembered the day. The little boy was wearing a white hat down over his eyes. Carrie, with her blond hair parted, and drawn back, tied with a fluttering strip of cloth. White pull-on shirt, white shorts, her limbs firm, her laughter free. Megan, the dark one, happy too that day, holding her child firmly before her, managing the horse with skill and strength.

The horses had seemed to be enjoying the fun as much as anyone. In the water, the girls had shouted back to Tuck on the shore. Would he come to their picnic? they asked. Oh, up the shore a way. They had rented a cabin up there — Carrie's hand waved vaguely to the north. For weekends this summer. They didn't realize that Tuck would be a neighbor.

He identified their cabin, a one-room, log deal, rented out to fishermen and people like the Reynolds girls, to ice fishermen in the winter. "It's better than five miles from my shack," he informed them.

The little boy, Bob, wanted to get down, and Tuck waded out to take him. Then Megan rode the horse up on the beach.

"Why didn't you do that in the first place?" Carrie asked, and followed suit.

The boy, Bob, was happy to be on the ground.

"This is Dr. Fairbairn," Megan formally introduced Tuck.

Both Tuck and Carrie protested. "The name's Tuck," the tall man said, squatting on his heels to bring himself to Bob's level.

"Horses stickle," said the child, rubbing his bare legs.

"They certainly do," Tuck agreed. "You run around for a bit and the stickles will go away." But as he watched the child run around, the laughter had faded away from his eyes. He glanced at Carrie, who questioned him with her eyes.

"I'll come to your picnic," he told the sisters. "And Bob can walk there with me. I'll tote him over the tired places."

The women departed, and Tuck endeavored to explain *tote* to Bob.

They had their picnic. Tuck joined the girls, Bob riding his shoulders, a tired little boy who refused all suggestions of a nap, but fell asleep in Megan's lap with his first hot dog half-eaten.

Carrie continued to search Tuck's face. But that day he said nothing. He did ask when they would be back. Only on weekends. Yes, Stowe might join them. But probably not. "He's a stiff old son of a gun," said Megan, laughing at this description of her lawyer husband.

Since Tuck's free day coincided with their use of the cabin, for the next month or so he went there regularly. He watched the little boy, he played with him, he took him swimming and felt of his limbs. They invented games. Bob would run down the path ahead of Tuck, and hide. Tuck would make a big deal of finding him.

They fished, they got tired and stretched out on the sun-warmed planks of the cabin's little pier. Carrie came to stand over them that time, and concern was ever darker in her eyes. For six weeks Tuck devoted his every free day to Bob. Of course he saw a lot of Carrie in the process, which was all gain. She was a comfortable person to be with; she suspected what he was doing but she let him take his own time to speak of it.

She was an exciting person to be with, too. She could match a man's moods, and be as silly as needed, as serious, as loving.

Carrie could remember, though Tuck could not, properly, when love had first been acknowledged between them. It had been a matter of firelight, on a late afternoon in the winter time. Carrie had agreed to come to see his cabin in the snow; she had explored it, they had taken a walk on cross-country skis, returning for the stew which had been cooking all day, toast made on long forks over the glowing logs, and apples roasted on a shovel. Their eyes met, their hands — their lips.

"I *know* where you have been all my life," Tuck told her. "But what was wrong with *me?*"

"Nothing is wrong with you, darling," she had told him.

"When you talk that way, I believe you. So tell me this. While I was warming up my engine, how come you didn't off and marry one of the hundred guys who must have asked you?"

She shrugged. "Maybe I was tending my traps," she told him, her eyes shining.

"Is that what you were doing? Working like a dog in o.r., letting me yell at you if someone dropped a forcep."

"You don't yell, Tuck."

"I do too yell. And since you've been o.r. head, I've yelled at you."

"Yes, doctor," she said primly.

He laughed, and caught her up into his arms.

"Tuck and Aunt Carrie get mushy sometimes," Bob told his mother.

"You get mushy with Carrie too, sometimes," Megan reminded him.

The child thought about this. "Well, yes, sometimes," he conceded.

"Don't you like it?"

His smile was wide. "Sure I do," he agreed. "And I guess Tuck likes it too."

A wonderful little boy.

"Stowe thinks he should call you Dr. Fairbairn," Carrie told him.

"Oh, gee, pops, Carrie!"

"He's stiff. Proper," Carrie agreed. "And Bob says, 'Oh, gee, pops!' too. Stowe shakes his head about *that!*"

"I wonder what he'll say when I tell him that his son should come into the hospital for examination and tests."

"He won't like it, and he might not agree to it."

"But, Carrie . . . we need to find out!"

"You're afraid of one of the *omas,* aren't you?"

"Myeloma, yes. But we'll wait and see what the examination shows."

Carrie looked down at the ground and shook her head. That day her thick and shining hair had been smoothly brushed and clubbed behind her head, tied there with a bow of rose velvet ribbon. Tuck had searched her eyes, his own earnestness betrayed in every line of his face, of his strong body. She touched the lapel of his tweed jacket, her fingertips brushed across the thick fisherman's sweater he wore. "We've been afraid . . ." she whispered.

"Then you can tell Megan, or I will, if you like. Stowe too, of course. What's wrong with that?"

She was shaking her head. "Oh, it's just that Stowe . . . He won't even admit that Bob limps."

"Well, he'll have to admit it! Sooner or later. The limp has grown worse in the past month."

"Ye-es."

"And we should know the reason for it. If you don't want me to tell him, if I, personally, am a factor . . ." Again he searched her eyes. "There are other doctors."

"Yes, and they would refer us right back to you."

"Us?" he repeated.

"Well, Megan and Stowe, of course. I'm only the maiden aunt."

He laughed. "You don't look like one."

"I am sure Megan wants to help the boy."

"Don't you imagine that Stowe does too?"

"If he thought Bob was sick."

"*If?*" Tuck's voice rose. "O.K. O.K. Would he take him to a pediatrician?"

"Well, maybe he would let Megan do it. Of course Bob has gone to a pediatrician before." Her face brightened. "Yes," she said. "I'll talk to her about that."

"Time is important, Carrie."

"Oh, I know that, Tuck. Of course I do."

So, this morning, finishing with the spine, going on to pin the kneecap, coming back to check on the cast which Dr. Shadrach had made for the spine case, then ready to take on the osteomyelitis, Tuck told Carrie that he wished it would be Bob coming to the table.

"It would mean more to me to help that boy than all five of today's cases, Carrie," he said roughly. "It's to help kids like him that I studied medicine, and have trained and trained as an orthopod."

Her dark eyes answered him, the brush of her hand across his sleeve.

But . . .

Tuck himself had been the one to ask Megan to bring Bob in for an examination.

"Because he limps," said Megan, her voice thin.

"Because of whatever it is that makes him limp, sweetheart."

She studied his grave face, she looked at Carrie. I trust you, Tuck," she told him. "And I — Carrie and I — have been afraid that something was seriously wrong."

"This should be attended to as soon as possible, Megan."

Carrie watched them, listened, white-faced.

"The trouble is," said Megan, "Stowe wouldn't hear of such a thing."

Though Carrie had suggested such a situation, Megan's speaking of it so firmly shocked Tuck. "But, *Megan!*" he cried. "Any father would want to help his child!"

"In theory, yes," Megan agreed. "Actually — do you know Stowe Vashon, Tuck?"

"No, I don't. I know I must have seen him. I went to your wedding . . . He must have been there. I may have seen him a time or two since. But, no, I don't know him. And of course he doesn't know me. But I still think that any father . . ."

"Let me tell you about Stowe," said Megan earnestly. "Maybe I can make you understand. You see — well, first, he has a lawyer's mind. He thinks in terms of thick yellow lawbooks, precedents, verdicts, decisions. All that. Second, in everything he does, in everything he has, Stowe strives for, and wants, perfection."

This angered Tuck. And it frightened him, as well. "What in hell does he think big hospitals are built for?" he cried.

"Not for *his* son. Never for his son, Tuck. He cannot, and will not, believe that his boy, his son, could have any crippling disease."

"But that's crazy!"

"It could be. But when I've tried to talk to him about it, he becomes so angry that I've been frightened. He gets angry at Carrie too. He says she is surgery-oriented, and all that."

"And the boy still needs attention," said Tuck grimly. "Not necessarily from me, Megan. Though I am close. And most certainly interested."

It had been bad, at the time when he had

talked to Megan, and since. This morning he *had* wished the child on the table could have been Bob; as he scrubbed after the lunch break he wished it would be Bob who now waited beyond the swinging doors into the operating room.

Dear God, he did not want Bob to need surgery any more than Stowe Vashon did! But if he did need it, and Tuck were given the chance, he would do his very, very best —

He certainly did wish that, in a day or two, he would be given the chance to care for the child.

Bob, who didn't want to be called Bobby. It was tragic that such a child should be touched with disaster. It was even more tragic, should that be possible, that Bob could be a matter of conflict between his parents, that his health must be. These happenings were never easy, but the loving understanding of the father and mother always helped the child.

And the doctor too, Tuck muttered as he took his place at the scrub basin, and thrust his arms and hands into the cone of bright water.

But Stowe and Megan —

Scrub, scrub. From hundreds of scrubs, Tuck could count automatically, and think of other things besides. Today he thought about Stowe and Megan Vashon. He still did did not know the husband at all. He had seen the man three or four times. Mainly at his wedding to Megan Reynolds. Ten years ago, for heaven's sake! Tuck closed his eyes, trying to pull up pictures. Many things were brighter in his memory than that bridegroom standing beside the bride. He was a tall man. His hair was the same reddish blond that Bob had, thick upon his head. His coat had fitted his shoulders superbly; the exact line of white showed above the collar. At the reception, young Dr. Tucker Fairbairn may or may not have gone down the receiving line. He did remember kissing Megan. All the hospital guys, residents, staff, and interns, had lined up to kiss her.

They had made a thing of her marrying a nonmedical character. And she had made a joke of not being able to choose among them. Laughing, bright-eyed, she had been beautiful on her wedding day. Tuck remembered *that!* Her veil had been of lace upon her soft brown hair, her gown had shimmered and glowed. Not a flat white, more like rich ivory . . .

A great many of the guests had been from the hospital. A favorite joke was to ask,

"Who's minding the store?"

But Megan Reynolds had been a Records clerk at the hospital for some time. Five years perhaps. Tuck could remember her there when he had been an intern. A slender, pretty girl with a frank, smiling way about her. One able to answer any medic's quip or jibe. She was extremely popular. Tuck Fairbairn had liked her a lot. He still did.

As a Records clerk, she had been a dandy. She made good money, her position in the hospital had been secure. Why then had she married a stubborn lawyer who didn't give her a child for six years, and then would not take care of that same child?

"You mad at something, Tuck?" Dr. Moore asked, joining him at the basin.

"At the world," Tuck answered him. "Donald, do you remember Megan Reynolds when she was a Records clerk here?"

"Sure I do. When she'd sit on the ladder and hunt for a file on some case ten years old, she had the prettiest legs in the place."

Tuck laughed, and squirted water at his assistant. "I might have known . . ." he conceded.

"She was a good clerk," Dr. Moore continued. "She helped me many times when I was a student. Everybody loved her. Insurance men, statisticians, legal beagles . . ."

"And she married one of those," Tuck said grimly.

'I remember that too. He came in here for a precedent on a damage case he had. Megan was great to him; he fell in love with her, and they were married."

"You know more than I do about the circumstances," growled Tuck, turning away from the basin.

"Maybe I knew her better. I was a student, then an intern, and had a lot of questions."

"I'll bet. Did you go to the wedding?"

Dr. Moore attended to his fingernails. "Hell, no," he drawled. "I worked that day. I sure did work that day. I was one of the interns, not knowing a damn thing, who were kept on duty. All you residents went to the wedding, and left the hospital at our mercy. It has never recovered."

"We're working on it," said Dr. Fairbairn, walking away from the round, stone-like basin.

But Megan most certainly had been a fine Records librarian. Tuck remembered at least one occasion, when he was studying in Europe, she had sent him transcripts of certain cases . . . She still must be a smart woman, and resourceful.

He went into the operating room where the elbow case was giving the anaesthetist a bit of trouble. Partially sedated, the boy did not want a cap on his head, he did not want to lie down . . .

Tuck refused to interfere. The team could handle this. Gowned, masked, towels folded around his hands, he went over to the lighted wall panels and studied the x-rays of the rambunctious youth's elbow. No doubt about his preference to work on Bob Vashon over this foul-mouthed kid.

Moore had been an intern . . . Moore was now laying down the law to their patient. And he had a vocabulary that surpassed that of the protester. The whole o.r. now listened in awe. Tuck Fairbairn smiled. Moore had always been one of many surprises.

Had he known Megan well enough to be invited to her parents' home for Sunday supper? Tuck had been, and he remembered the occasions with warmth and gratitude. Both parents were now dead, the old house torn down to make room for a supermarket, which still seemed a desecration, but back then, ten years ago, the rambling house had glowed with firelight and lamplight, had smelled deliciously of the lentil soup, or the baked beans. There was nothing fancy about the food at those suppers. But a never-empty bowl of hot soup, slabs of homemade bread with butter and sometimes honey, molasses cookies, and literally buckets of hot cocoa — iced tea in the summer time — had been wonderful. The place roared with the loud talk, and had rocked with laughter. It had been a sad day when Megan had married and left the hospital.

When Tuck had eaten soup at the Reynoldses', Carrie had been little more than a child. A pretty young girl of twelve, thirteen, or so, with sun-streaked yellow hair, huge dark, dark blue eyes, and a skin he had never seen equaled except in England. It seemed that a light glowed behind it. She was a cute girl, but just a kid among all the smarty medics in their twenties. They were kind to her, teased her — Tuck himself had teased her, she claimed, but she also remembered that he had proven to her that he could too french-braid her hair, which was longer then, and like fine silk against his fingers.

"I knew you would make a wonderful surgeon," she now told Tuck. "Your hands were so strong, and yet light of touch. You didn't pull, or jerk my head around."

That evening had been fun. All the evenings were. The doctors who had attended them must remember them warmly, gratefully. They would remember Megan's wedding, too. The regular visitors to the Reynolds home had all been invited. Tuck got back from Europe just in time to attend. And to find that Carrie was growing up to be a lovely young woman. Sixteen then. Seventeen? Her skin still like porcelain, her eyes shaded by thick lashes, her voice soft.

Tuck had stood in a corner and stared at her. He resented her growing up so soon. She was still too young — and he became angry at the talk he heard, the gossip, really, to the effect that everyone had thought Stowe Vashon was in love with Megan's younger sister.

This had shocked Tuck. Carrie? He searched the crowd for another look at that young sister.

Well — she was going to be a raving beauty, when she did grow up. Now she still had the petal bloom of genuine youth. Yes, she was poised. For her age. She could talk easily to the men who were guests, and to the women as well. Megan's friends, her parents' friends.

But her bridesmaid's dress of pale blue thin stuff had been the dress of a younger girl, her wide-brimmed hat, her demure, lace-edged bouquet was not the sort of thing that would be carried by a young woman old enough to attract her sister's lover.

Oh, *attract* was the wrong word. Carrie was so deliciously lovely that she would *attract* anyone.

But the things being said . . .

"Mrs. Reynolds liked the girls to do things together. Dates, even . . ."

"And Vashon loved it. He always danced with Carrie. Several times."

"Why didn't he marry her?"

"*That* wasn't Megan's plan. Besides, Carrie was too young. She still is."

"Then — ?"

"Never underestimate the power of a woman ready to claim a man."

"I guess one shouldn't."

Tuck had listened, he had heard. But he had not believed. Gossip was the breath of life for hospital people. He had not believed the gossip, but he had heard it, and now he remembered it. It was all a part of his having known Megan — and Carrie. The Reynolds parents, their home, their friends. Hot bean soup, gingerbread, and cocoa.

Stowe could not have come to the Sunday evening parties, and those were the only times Tuck spent at the big frame house. He had been abroad for several years, and after his return to the Complex as a junior staff member, Tuck had not gone there.

But he remembered the family . . . he now remembered the teasing talk to the girls, and about them. He —

Someone touched his arm, and he brought himself back to the present, to the now-passive patient on the table and the shattered elbow prepped for the surgeon's delicate handiwork. He perched on a stool and went to work.

Megan and Carrie, their home, their parents still drifted through his thoughts. Mrs. Reynolds was a small woman, but intense in all she did. The father was a big, smiling man, with Carrie's clear, fair skin, and the family genius for making friends. They were people who did almost everything as a group. The father was an engineer for the Complex; Megan had got her job through him, and through Megan, Carrie was planning on nursing school. Their mother had learned to talk what she called medicalese. She could play games with her girls and her husband, and their friends. Such travel as they did was together, the four of them. Such entertaining was . . . the Sunday evening suppers. Tuck supposed that Megan, at least, had had dates of her own. Carrie must have shared high school affairs — sock hops, picnics, slumber parties, and proms.

Megan's work in the Records room, Tuck would have said, was her main interest in life. She liked men, exchanged jokes with them, helped the doctors, and enjoyed talking to them, having coffee with one or the other of them in the lounge. She was a beautiful and clever girl. And the knowledge she had of the hospital records was phenomenal. She must have enjoyed the job to be so very good at it.

She was given credit for her help in establishing the two four-year training schools for record librarians in their city. One-year courses were afforded high school graduates who wanted to train as record technicians. She was indomitable in her insistence that all records be complete in every detail, and was a bloodhound in tracking down the people who should make that record complete.

She liked to call herself and her department the ones who could solve any mystery case that reached the hospital. "Every clue is right there in those stacks of files, or they darn well better be." No one, Tuck believed, had ever expected her to give up the work she loved and believed in so completely.

Her affair with Vashon must have worked up very quickly. "When my back was turned," Tuck told himself at the time, and now still believed. Of course he had turned his back. Studying at other medical centers, then busy doing staff work at the Complex, joining the staff of a second hospital in the city, deciding on the specialty of bone disease diagnosis and treatment.

"And there was the age bit," he admitted, pushing his stool away from the table to let Moore close and dress the repaired elbow. The need to prove to himself and others that he was a genius doctor.

"I need a breath of air," he told his assistant. "We have one more job?"

"I'm afraid so."

The wall clock said 4 P.M. Tuck stretched his back and arm muscles. "Then I'll be back," he said, pushing the tight cap from his head.

He pulled a white jacket over his green scrub suit and went to see his post-ops in I.C.U. All were doing well, though he would bet the spine would turn up peritonitis.

Then he stepped into the elevator and rode up to the roof, fishing his watch out of his sock so that he could check on the time. He should relax and take a quick nap. But he was on this think-gig . . .

"Fifteen minutes to think about my ego bit," he said wryly.

He stretched out on a chaise. This was a small area set off by screening glass and plants from the patients' roof lounge. Usually Tuck enjoyed looking out over the city, the tall buildings, the glint of dancing waters in the lakes.

Today, bone-tired, he stretched out and closed his eyes.

Every doctor, he imagined, went through what he called the ego bit. Having attained a certain level of success, staff positions, teaching schedules, a specialty, his own office, his own income — a swelling of the ego was all a part of it. Tuck had gone through the symptoms, the disease, and, he hoped, the cure. But there for a time it had preoccupied his full time and attention.

And it must have been during that time that Megan had given enough of her time and attention to meet Stowe Vashon. Tuck simultaneously had decided that he no longer had time for Sunday night soup and the game of categories at the Reynolds' home. Had he gone there at all? And possibly met Stowe? Possibly, but he really did not think that he had. At the wedding, yes, he had seen him. And not more than briefly since. He doubted if he would recognize

Vashon should the man come up here and sit down in the next chair. He really didn't think he would. Even though Tuck and Carrie were planning — that had all come to a head this summer, and Stowe wasn't staying at the cabin on weekends.

"He hates mosquitoes and ticks, and things," Megan had explained. "Though he felt it would be good for me and Bob to get fresh air and sunshine."

So Tuck did not know Stowe Vashon, then or now. He had heard about him. Through Megan's work, Carrie Reynolds had decided to go into nursing. Tuck had let his name be used as reference when she applied. Because she was so pretty, so full of life, he had enjoyed seeing her in the halls of the hospital. When it was his turn to conduct a class for the student nurses, he had lectured to Carrie Reynolds. He remembered her as a probie, he remembered when she had done her stint in orthopedics, and he made unwarranted claims on his friendship with her. This came to be a gag on the wards. But she was lovely, and she was going to make a great nurse.

"If she can keep her hands off her sister's man," said someone.

"Or his off her," someone else had corrected.

Tuck had been interested enough to inquire, and he heard Stowe's name coupled with Carrie's. He kept hearing things. Stories, some of which he did not believe. Carrie was not the sort to cut in on Megan. She was not the sort to shove her duties around so that she could "do" a weekend in Chicago with Megan's husband.

"He'd rather be Carrie's husband," was asserted.

Tuck heard these things and became angry. Enough to protest. "She's just a kid," he had said. And those gossiping about her had laughed at him; they were ready to supply him with particulars. "You can see her," he was told. "Out on the lake with the guy . . . on the ski run . . . in the back row at the movies."

That last did it. The other fellows were riding him, and he had better let them know that the game was over.

"Maybe I should look more closely," he had managed to say coolly.

But for a while his anger stayed with him. He supposed it had dissolved when the other doctors dropped the subject, and he became ever more deeply involved in his work.

But at the wedding, the stories had been hinted at, some were the same stories, some different. It was concluded by the medics that Megan was not being very nice to her younger sister.

"Oh," said someone, "Carrie isn't in love with Vashon."

"Maybe not. But I am sure he has been in love with her."

"And so he marries Megan."

"Oh, no. *She* is marrying him!"

As a group, the doctors called that distinction ridiculous. Tuck being one of them.

It was ridiculous, and he would forget about it. He decided that he knew the girls better than most of these fellows did. Theirs was too close a family for intrigue, schemes, and jealousies.

So — he had buried himself in his own affairs. Mainly in his work. Techniques were being developed in diagnosis and treatment of bone diseases; he developed some of his own. Such things kept him on his toes, they kept him busy.

Occasionally he considered marriage. Not to any special girl; it was just vaguely in his plans. A thing a man in his thirties should do. He built and enjoyed his "cabin." He saw Carrie fairly often; she was doing floor nursing and not in ortho. When Mrs. Reynolds died and the father of the family soon afterward, he sent flowers, and planned to call at the house. But something came up, and he was shocked, shortly afterward — actually two years afterward — to drive past the old house and find that it had disappeared.

He did ask Carrie about that. Megan, she said, had her own home. "I live in an apartment."

"May I come to see you sometime?"

"Of course."

But he had not, right away.

And he still did not know Stowe Vashon.

Well, none of that mattered now. Carrie was working in ortho, Tuck saw her all the time, and had urged her to help him in o.r. They both liked that. And now, Carrie loved him and would marry him — tomorrow if he would insist. Though of course both wanted the matter of Bob handled, settled. Carrie had said enough for him to understand that Stowe was at odds with her over the boy.

But, just maybe, some of his feeling could be over Tuck. And if that was holding things up, Dr. Fairbairn must withdraw from the case at once. Bob's health was the only thing that mattered! And it was the only thing he was going to think about, too. Though what a real gig of reminiscence he had been on all day!

He wished the whole thing had kept itself buried. He wished he had not been forced to acknowledge to himself that — even today — he believed that Stowe had once loved Carrie, and would have eventually married her. But before that eventuality had become accomplished — long before it — the wedding invitations came out. Megan was going to marry this Stowe Vashon. Dr. Tucker Fairbairn was invited to the ceremony, and to the reception which would follow.

Tuck had been surprised. Initially, that the wedding was to take place, and that it was to take place in three weeks. His surprise was almost as great that he should be invited. Lately he hadn't been all that close to the Reynoldses. Of course, once he had been . . .

He bought and sent a proper wedding gift. He made arrangements to attend — to see what had happened while his back was turned. Though he never had really found that out.

To this day, he was not sure just why Megan and this Stowe Vashon . . .

"This has been a day!" declared Donald Moore an hour and a half later, when he and his Chief could strip off their gloves, their caps and masks, shrug out of their surgical gowns, and go to the surgeons' lounge. "Do your feet hurt as much as mine do?"

"I no longer have any feet, Moore. Nor legs. But I sure do have a back, and all above it."

"You bet. How do you suppose Billings' throat is?"

Tuck snorted. "If I did have legs, I'd go to his house and find out," he said positively. "Though of course the time may come when you or I might have to do as he did . . ."

"I can't foresee that."

"It can happen. And we really did not need a strep throat in o.r. today."

"We didn't. But I call Billings lazy."

"He is lazy. But usually when he schedules three jobs in a day, it's because he needs the money."

"And he wouldn't cancel out for an itty-bitty rough throat."

Tuck got up out of his chair to fetch more coffee. "Donald," he said, returning, "I have spent today deciding that things can whiz by me without my knowing what fanned my back hair."

"Oh? What kind of things?"

"Well, lately, I've had the Reynolds girls on my mind."

"I've noticed."

"A-huh. I am old enough, you know, to get married."

Dr. Moore polished his eyeglasses. "Plenty old," he conceded. "And as of now you have five reports to make completely enough to satisfy the Records gals Megan Reynolds trained to be nit pickers and comma noticers."

"I'll have your help," said Tuck smoothly.

His assistant groaned. "I think I'll drown myself in the shower."

"I just may join you. But while we wait for the circulation to start up in our extremities, do you know, and can you tell me, just how, when, and why Megan Reynolds suddenly, or so it seemed to me at the time — why she suddenly married Stowe Vashon."

"Good Lord, man, that was years ago."

"And you think I've just forgotten?"

"Well — the whole hospital talked about the reason."

"Not to me. Or I have forgotten. But now I want to know."

"Because of their little boy."

"That's right. Bob. So refresh my memory."

Dr. Moore nodded, and glanced around the room. The o.r. team had all showered, dressed, and departed. An orderly was picking up litter, but orderlies didn't really care what the doctors talked about.

"Well," he began, "I never knew Vashon myself."

"I have that same problem. Except at the wedding, I doubt if I've ever seen the man."

Dr. Moore looked at him sharply.

Tuck shrugged. "One of my present problems is a father who won't talk to the doctor, or vice versa."

"Good Lord, Tuck! Won't he?"

"Ug-ugh. So go back ten years."

"Well, he was a lawyer. Still is, I presume."

"He is."

"Yes. And there was a lawsuit. A rather spectacular one against a doctor right here in this hospital."

"Skull and Bones wasn't built then, but that's all right. Continue."

"I meant the Complex. The doctor was an o.b.-gyn fella. Big shot. You must remember that!"

"Thrombosis? Anybody can throw a thrombus. Anybody can die like snuffing out a candle."

"They can, and this patient did. The doctor was a very prominent, popular, successful man. In his field, and in this city. The lawsuit immediately became a spectacular case — you must have been out of the country."

"I've decided that I was. Go on."

"It was talked up here, and in society. Literally, this successful man's career and future were at stake."

"Besides . . ."

"Yes. Anybody can throw a thrombus."

"All right. We know that. But the courts didn't, the juries didn't. So this doctor needed a lawyer, and the firm selected to represent him delegated Stowe Vashon to do the investigation. And I will say he worked like the devil on it."

"With Megan's help."

"Oh, yes. Because his line was what we have mentioned. Anybody could throw a clot — anybody can die — but mostly people accept the doctor's explanation — mostly people understand that there are limits to a doctor's ability to save lives.

"Anyway, the investigation went on, and Stowe had lots of chances to be with Megan, to notice her pretty legs, to be grateful to her . . ."

"And she would help him."

"Oh, yes. She could pull those manila

folders out, and out . . . She found cases where this same doctor had used the identical procedures and the patient survived. It was all there in black and white that this same woman had successfully borne two other children. Megan then found the records of four doctors who had attended mothers of two previous children, with episiotomies, but no thrombosis. Then they found cases of other thrombus . . ."

"And no lawsuits."

"That's right."

"I see. Megan could produce all that evidence."

"I'll say. Whatever the lawyers wanted, she could pull those manila folders out, and out. Of course, the hospital wanted to be cleared, too."

"Of course. Was Vashon rather young to be given such an important case?"

"Well, he was and he wasn't. He had been something of a prodigy, you know."

"No, that's what I don't know. For all I know of the man myself, he could be a scarecrow in a farmer's field."

Dr. Moore's attention sharpened. "You really haven't seen him? Talked to him about Bob?"

"No, I haven't. He won't admit that anything is wrong. And I cannot understand why a father should act that way. This puzzling has set me thinking back to what has been going on in that family."

"I see. Carrie should know."

"She probably does, though she hasn't lived with them, and Vashon resents her attempts to get the boy into my clutches."

"Oh, now, *doctor!*"

"I may have to tell them to take him elsewhere. Maybe even out of the city."

"I'd hope not."

"Yes. So tell me about this fella."

"Where was I? Oh, yes. Vashon at the time Megan was helping him to find precedents in this prodigious lawsuit."

"You said he had been a prodigy."

"He was. Admitted to the bar when he was twelve or something."

Tuck made a gesture of being ready to leave, of abandoning the discussion. Dr. Moore laughed. "O.K. O.K.," he apologized. "He was young, not very handsome, but distinguished-looking."

"Do you still know him?"

"I never did know him well. He was put on that malpractice case, and through Megan's help he could pile up evidence so that he was able to do a very good job on his briefs, or whatever their prognosis evaluations are called."

"This was before he married Megan."

"Oh, yes. Besides, at the time, actually —"

"I know about that. He was said to be in love with Carrie."

"Yes, there was that talk. But Carrie was only sixteen or seventeen then. A perfectly delightful girl. She still is, Tuck."

"I know she is. But if —"

"Megan moved pretty fast back then," said Dr. Moore quickly. "But she had been ready to work hard. It must have taken weeks, mostly after hours, to dig out all those files. She was pretty, and she was clever — but the main thing was, she knew exactly what to do to give old stone-face Stowe Vashon a way to win his big case."

"With precedents."

"Yes, because they were evidence. But there was still another angle. The husband had sworn, you could remember, that the o.b.'s postnatal care had been less than it should have been. That he had done various things, and failed to do others — I forget the details. And our girl Megan had other files. This same husband, sometime before, had been psycho'd and proven to be a psychopathic, congenital liar. And the lie detector tests he offered to take at the time of the thrombosis suit didn't mean a thing because it had been proven — Megan could find these proofs too — it had been proven that psycho-liars could breeze through a lie detector's questions and show no reaction. They could fool a machine, because lies meant nothing to them. Some doctor on our staff had made a study of that, and written a paper or two. Megan knew where to find *that!* Oh, she was a busy little girl.

"The suing lawyers thought they could lick the precedent evidence by the husband's testimony, and his performance on the lie machine. But when it turned out that this same man — the husband — had been labeled a congenital liar in our Psych department —"

"The case fell apart. Because Megan had those records too."

"Yes, she did. Of course there still is discussion as to whether the evidence would have stood up in court before a jury, but what mattered was that it sufficed to get the suit withdrawn, which is the only way any doctor ever wins a malpractice suit, Tuck."

Tuck pulled his height up out of the low chair. "You're so right," he groaned. "I think I'm ready to shower."

"A-hmmmm. I'll help you with the reports."

"Yes, and make rounds with me."

"Oh, now, look . . ."

"I trust the resident. But I check my own post-ops."

Dr. Moore knew that he did.

"The development was a big thing for Stowe Vashon," he shouted over the noise of the two showers. "Your Carrie told all about it at the wedding, don't you remember that?"

"I don't think I hung around that wedding very long. I remember how she looked . . ."

I'm told she was enchanting. And naïve about how wonderful she thought Megan had been, and Stowe too. I also heard several people declare that the suit's withdrawal had and would set Vashon up in his profession."

"And Stowe was grateful to Megan, and married her."

Dr. Moore laughed, and wielded a large towel. "That wasn't the whole of it, Tuck. There's more."

Tuck pushed his head through his turtleneck sweater and waited, his eyes on Moore, who was combing his hair. "What more?" He nudged the other man.

"We're gossiping like two old women."

"So, we gossip. And this day is getting damn long."

"Yes, it is, isn't it? Well, I never did know the precise facts on the Megan-Stowe story, but we young bucks had some clues, and we did our own gossiping, and rather figured out what had happened. Then, at the wedding, there was Carrie, all flushed and excited."

And her hat kept slipping back on her head, and she was so *pretty!*

"She wanted to tell everyone."

"And good manners made everyone listen."

Dr. Moore flushed.

"Yes," Tuck agreed. "I want to know too."

"You could figure the thing out."

"I probably have. But what did Carrie tell?"

"I was not there, but I understand she thought everything was wonderful. The kid didn't know that Stowe was in love with *her.* I asked enough questions to be very sure of that, Tuck. She looked on him only as an older brother. We fellows all decided that."

"Go on," said Tuck. "Tell me."

"If Carrie remembers what she said that day, she probably regrets it."

"But she'd drunk too much champagne."

"That was part of it. Excitement made her more reckless than the wine did, I suspect. Because it seems that she did chatter. I can imagine . . ."

"So can I," said Tuck dryly.

"All right, sir. I'll talk. First, she assured everyone that the result of the malpractice suit had definitely set Stowe up in his profession. He was in line for a partnership. Then . . ."

Donald Moore talked, and Tuck listened to the story which young Carrie had told to her fascinated listeners. From that story, Tucker Fairbairn could imagine what really had happened. The events seemed plausible enough; they would be explained by what he knew of Megan and Stowe.

Stowe Vashon must have been grateful to Megan. He surely had been. The natural thing would have been for him to say to Miss Reynolds, "Let's celebrate."

She had agreed, as triumphant as he was, and their celebration had expanded to a weekend in Chicago. Perhaps anything beyond that had not been in Vashon's plans. But he did owe Megan a lot, and ten years ago, a man, faced with a shocked set of parents, felt certain obligations. He went through with the results of the "situation," which was what the Reynolds parents evidently had called the development, and scandal was lost in the unexpected announcement of the engagement, with the wedding set for a month later, with the issuing of the wedding invitations.

Tuck could remember getting his, and being surprised. Yes, there had been talk, and excitement. Megan was very popular in the Complex, and her marriage to this lawyer was not to be expected. He well remembered Carrie, lovely as a young bridesmaid, herself triumphant at the way things had turned out; fate, she said, had let Megan find and get the man she wanted. He remembered Carrie because, during the ceremony, he had watched the young girl, big-eyed and exquisitely beautiful.

And, unwillingly, almost too vividly, he remembered the brief scene at the reception on which he had stumbled. They had stood by an open window, hidden somewhat by a tall vase of flowers, and Stowe was looking down at Carrie, his back to the room. His finger tipped her face up, and swiftly he had bent to kiss the girl's soft cheek. It was a swift and tender minute. Tuck had turned away from it. But someone else had seen it too. A man, a friend, who had come to join Tuck, and had seen the two together. "I always thought," said this man, "any wedding would be between those two."

So Tuck did remember Stowe Vashon from the wedding.

"Let's get at those reports," he said now, brusquely, to Dr. Moore. "I'll do mine, you take Billings'."

Dr. Moore made no comment.

"I know there are three in that bundle," Tuck threw over his shoulder. He sounded angry. Then he relaxed. "I'm giving you an extra one as pay for a good story."

They went to the desk, and began to fill in the reports. "It was a good story," he conceded shortly.

Dr. Moore nodded. "After the fellas got over the champagne, they decided that most of it was true."

"Anyway, it worked," said Tuck. "If there was a scheme."

Moore finished one report, and fastened it into the chart. "You're not turning these cases back to Billings, are you?"

"And get sued for malpractice? Not me. Donald, when I get married, it's going to be because I love the girl."

"That's a good way," Dr. Moore agreed. "Do you think Megan maybe would agree with us?"

"I hope her marriage wasn't — hasn't been — pure hell."

Dr. Moore was busily writing.

"It probably has not been," Tuck concluded. "The two of them do have Bob."

Three

For all of the rest of that week, Dr. Fairbairn continued to be extremely busy. This sort of situation always irritated him. He tried never to take on more cases than he could handle by steady, and hard, work, careful examinations and thought, with time to give of himself to the patient and to the patient's family. Time for careful research on each case, careful examinations and always, always careful thought.

But for that whole week, starting with Billings' three cases dumped into his o.r. schedule, things did seem to pile up for him. He saw patients, he attended consultations and staff meetings, he conducted classes and demonstrations. On two of those days he did scheduled surgery. The spine fusion case which he had done on that first busy day did develop peritonitis, and he concerned himself with that.

Twice during that week he was tempted not to go to his cabin at night, but the woods, the lake, and being alone always rested and refreshed him.

On Saturday he was still preoccupied by the appearance of a rare salmonella infection which seemed to have originated in the Complex's own blood supply. The doctors, of course, had to use commercial blood, and platelets were so damn fragile . . . Tuck's shoulders could scream from fatigue before the doctors could think themselves even close to identifying the donor who was behind the case of chloerae-suis he seemed to have been handed by a colleague. By Friday night, one donor had been located who could have given the salmonella platelets to each of the seven cases under consideration. Not, of course, all of them in his hospital. This fifty-year-old professional blood donor claimed to be in perfect health. On Monday, if necessary, Tuck would determine if he was, or was not . . . Meanwhile, they had two bags of this man's blood; they would culture it over the weekend.

And for this Saturday morning, at least, Tuck could put on a warm jacket and heavy shoes and walk through the woods, clear to where a spring-fed creek poured its icy waters down the hillside toward the lake. "I'll bet that donor has an osteomyelitis somewhere," he addressed the undergrowth through which he pushed. "Most osteos hurt — he'd be one of the stubborn ones who ignores pain. I'll bet —"

The waters of the creek raced jade green and white between the wooded slopes, now leaf-strewn in the early sunlight. The sound which the swift waters made drowned out any other possible noise, and after a time Tuck found his head held higher, his shoulders relaxing, his eyes seeing only the patterns which the tree branches made against the blue-white sky. He wished he could paint and catch the play of light on the dark rocks, the bronze green colors of the deep pools, and the silvery crest of the current. Watching for a place to cross the stream, he did not see Megan until she spoke to him.

"Tucker Fairbairn, will you *wait* for me?" she cried. "You walk so fast . . ."

He turned in surprise. "What are you doing here?" he demanded.

"Same thing you are. Trying not to slip on these rocks."

He extended his hand.

"I want to talk to you," she said, safely beside him.

"I meant, what are you doing out here in the woods?"

"We came up here yesterday afternoon. We give up our shack in ten days or so. I thought this would be my best chance to talk to you."

"What about?"

"I think you know what about, Tuck. I want you to examine Bob, and give me an opinion that will let me sleep at nights."

"I couldn't guarantee that, Megan."

There were smoky smudges under her dark eyes. "I know you can't, Tuck. But at least we'd *know!* This thing of worried imaginings . . ."

He had led her away from the creek's edge, and now they could stand and talk, with the sunlight touching their heads and shoulders. "Have you persuaded your husband . . . ?" he asked.

Her eyes searched his. "No, I haven't," she said frankly.

"Then I can't take the case, Megan. You know that."

She did know it, of course, and readily said so. "I am not suggesting that you perform surgery without Stowe's consent. But I have to know if anything is wrong with my son, and your face has told me that you think there is something wrong. Can't you examine him and — ?"

"I can, and will, suggest that you take him to another surgeon for those tests and examinations, dear."

Her hand clutched the sleeve of his jacket. "Tuck," she said tensely, "I am dreadfully afraid that he needs *you!*"

Megan was dark where Carrie was as blond as an angel. Megan's hair was a cap of crow's feathers on her head. Her eyes were also dark blue, but heavily shadowed by thick eyelashes and brows. Her lips were full, and red, and this morning they trembled.

She did not mention Carrie's name, nor did Tuck. He did not need to. He was swiftly thinking back over the summer weeks, to the day when he had first seen Bob. The lake water had sparkled like diamonds, and swirled froth around the horses' legs; and the little boy's big eyes had regarded him somberly from under the wide brim of a ridiculous hat. Tuck had watched the child run along wooded paths; he had taught him to swim, and had felt of his legs. He knew something was wrong; he knew that he should find out just how wrong . . .

"I'll talk to Carrie," he said now to Megan. "Whatever I decide will involve her. I should have her advice. She understands your position and she will understand mine."

"I understand it too, Tuck," said Megan earnestly.

"How would we manage even the examination and tests?"

"Without Stowe's knowing? He knows I've brought Bob up here with Carrie to get the place ready to turn back next week. He hates the woods; he said right at the beginning that we'd not get him up here."

"Bob will chatter about the hospital."

"Yes, he will. But by then we'd have something to tell Stowe."

"I don't like this, Megan."

"I know you don't. But talk to Carrie — she wants you to care for Bob. Oh, Tuck, please!"

He turned and walked with her back among the trees to the road which led to her cabin. He bent and kissed her cheek. "Tell Carrie I'll pick her up around four," he said, and turned back into the woods.

He came to the rented shack at precisely four, bringing with him a toy for Bob to divert the child from his announced intention of going on a picnic with Carrie and Tuck. Bob sharply detected the ploy but decided that today he would use his bright yellow bulldozer, and go on the next picnic.

Carrie and Tuck both were laughing when they drove away. "How did he know there was to be a picnic?" Tuck asked, avoiding a chuck hole.

"Every meal out here in the woods is a picnic," she told him.

"Well, that's just about my idea of it too," Tuck agreed.

Carrie settled down with her hand on the sleeve of his leather jacket. A red and white scarf tied her hair; she wore a red sweater with a white blouse and slender black slacks.

"I thought the pond . . ." he said tentatively.

The pond was a small inlet of Tuck's lake; there were flat rocks, and he would have brought cushions and blankets. "That will be fine," she said softly.

They talked about the weather. They talked about the cholerae-suis case — she was sure Tuck was on the right track. "You been peeping at the Petri dishes?" he asked.

"I left Skull and Bones before you did yesterday."

He knew she had. He always checked. "I thought maybe, tomorrow, we could look at a house I might buy for us."

"I like your cabin just fine."

"We'll keep it for weekends. But I can't have the little tads falling in the lake, or even down the stairs from the bedroom. This house . . ."

In spite of her efforts to divert him, he

talked about the house, and their plans. He would not let her say one word about Bob until they were at the "pond," and were ready to open the picnic basket which he had brought.

"The burnished gold of autumn," said Carrie contentedly when he sat down beside her on the flat blue cushion which he had laid on the rocks.

He hummed a contented agreement, and put his arm around her. "*Shhhh,*" he said, "let's listen to twilight fall."

She laughed silently, and laid her head into the hollow of his shoulder. Burnished gold, indeed. The water rippled gently, a bird murmured sleepily. For the two people seated there so silently, seeming not to breathe, senses quickened, hearing sharpened. Their eyes adjusted to the reduced light as pools of darkness gathered between the old trees. "I smell more sharply," Tuck whispered. Carrie's fingers pressed his lips to silence. She pointed to the v-shaped ripples following as ducks and geese silently coursed over the water. Water and sky now were colors melting from pink to red and mauve. A family group of small geese sailed effortlessly in line; a single duck made a narrow path. Two geese pushed sleepily by, their tails high, their necks lowered.

Carrie stirred. "We have to talk," she murmured.

He rose, lit the lantern, and opened the picnic basket. There was wine, and hot coffee in an enormous Thermos. There were little crisp knots of lettuce hearts, and paper-thin sandwiches of chicken and of moist sweet jam, chunks of cheese.

"Some drippy peaches for later," he promised.

"You think of everything," she agreed. "Can we talk now?"

"We've been talking for the past hour."

"I know. About Petri dishes and the advantages of carpeting over tile floors. About whether I'll work after we are married."

"Our first fight may be when I say no to that," he promised.

"It could be. I'll hate to leave you alone in o.r."

"It's just so I can have you alone in b.r. That means —"

She giggled. "Don't tell me. I know the line that mind of yours takes. But seriously, Tuck —"

He finished the sandwich in his hand, and dusted his fingers. "I know," he agreed. "Bob. Megan explained the setup you've devised."

"Darling . . ."

He leaned forward to pick up his mug of wine. "I've decided to admit him next week, Carrie," he said gruffly. "For tests."

She gasped, she gulped, and then she leaned her head forward to her knees.

Tuck watched her in amazement. "Tell me," he said, "what you would have done if I had said no."

She laughed, then, and wiped her cheeks with the back of her hand. And he kissed her. "Just tests," he said then. "Some of them will be painful."

"Tuck, do you think . . . ?"

"I'm not ready for any sort of diagnosis," he reminded her.

"But —"

"Eat your sandwich. And tell me what you have told Stowe about all this. Megan says he thinks she and the boy are out at the lake for several days."

"Yes. For as much as ten days. Closing a cabin takes time."

"And so do the tests we will make. But once those ten days are used up, and the family goes home, Bob is going to chatter like a monkey about hospitals and machines, needles, and nurses, not to mention his friend Tuck in a white gown."

Carrie sat silent. Then: "I know, dear," she said meekly. "But I can tell from your face that you are afraid . . ."

"Damn right I'm afraid! *For* the boy, and *of* his father."

"But the boy is the most important. The first day you saw him, you showed concern."

"As to why the little fellow limped. Even if I were not in the profession, I would have been concerned. Healthy little boys don't run with a limp. And that little boy, in the past weeks, has developed an unmistakable limp. There's tenderness. I am sure his father knows something is wrong with his leg."

"He may know, but he sharply resents any suggestion that the boy, his son, could be crippled."

"How long . . . ?"

"I first noticed it early last spring. I suggested the cabin in the woods where Bob could get lots of sunshine and good air. Stowe accepted that, not mentioning the limp."

"He's afraid."

"Yes, and that makes him stubborn, and angry."

"Well, his attitude makes me frightened, and damned angry too."

"Oh, I know, Tuck —"

"These cases are never easy, Carrie. You

know they are not. But with father and mother to sustain the child . . . Think of him, Carrie. Think of *him!*"

"Oh, I do, Tuck. I do."

"There are times when I get the idea . . . If I am the problem, Carrie . . ."

"You're not, Tuck. You couldn't be. But we did have to manage to get the child examined."

"All right, all right. I've known patients' families to scheme and plot. But I can tell you right now, I am going to insist on Stowe Vashon being present when I tell you what we find."

She said nothing. Tuck watched her anxiously. "Carrie?" he asked finally.

She lifted her head, and drew a deep breath. "You suggested — you asked if Stowe might have some feelings against you."

"And you asked how he could."

"I know I did. But he — he knows I work with you, that we plan to be married . . ."

"And he might think I would influence you to have the child . . ."

"If — if he takes a dislike to you, Tuck, would you abandon Bob's case?"

"No. I'd turn it over to Moore."

"Megan would never allow that."

He pounded his fist on his knee. "It's getting time," he said tightly, "when I should do some allowing myself!"

She got to her knees. "Oh, Tuck, darling!" she cried, "you are frightened."

"I am troubled. I want this thing done right. It could mean all the difference to Bob. And he's what matters."

"Yes," she said softly. "Of course he is."

"And things are not right. I already regret my agreement to go behind the door this way."

"Oh, Tuck!"

"I just don't do that sort of medicine, Carrie! You know that I don't. Why can't you people just make an appointment with a pediatrician who would surely refer Bob. You could arrange that, love, right within the Complex. You know you could."

"That's right," she agreed. "Except that I can't do it."

"You can tell Megan to do it, can't you?"

"I can tell her. In fact, I have told her. She takes Bob to the doctor if he has a cold. Why can't she attend to this in the same way? But she says she can't, and I believe her."

"Because of Stowe Vashon."

"That's it. Because of Stowe."

Tuck unwrapped sandwiches for them both, and filled their coffee mugs.

"Do you know Stowe, Tuck?" Carrie asked. "I mean —"

"I don't believe I have seen the man since Megan's wedding. And I didn't *know* him then. What's more, he doesn't know me."

"Megan has talked about that. She says if you and I really are going to be married . . ."

"When, not if. And we sure as thunder are going to be married."

"Yes, we are. Megan was thinking of asking us to have dinner with them."

"When I can make the guy mad by telling him his child needs medical care. A fine party that would be."

"Megan and I thought of that. So — you were not invited."

"And the kid still needs medical care. I need not tell you, Carrie, that in these cases, time is very important. Megan should get that child to the doctors while something still can be done for the boy."

Now Carrie sat silent. Tuck watched her in the flickering of the lantern. She ate her chicken sandwich, she picked up her coffee mug. Then she glanced at him.

"Stowe," she said slowly, "thinks you are capable of witch hunting."

"What on earth does that mean?"

"He feels that way about all doctors. He

suspects that Megan and I have talked to you about Bob. And of course the child says things about seeing you out here at the lake. You taught him to dog-paddle. He says, 'Oh, gee, pops!' the way you do. Stowe asked him where he'd got the phrase. Bob told him, vividly. You have been big in his life these past weeks."

"I see. And the father is jealous."

"He's angry because he suspects Megan and I have talked to you about Bob's health."

Tuck groaned. "Oh, fine! You really have set me up, Carrie."

"I know we have, darling," she said earnestly. "Not meaning to, or wanting to. Stowe jumps on the slightest thing!"

"He must be a thoroughly charming person."

"Well, actually he is. He can be. He used to be. But he does not like the idea of some other man being responsible for the child he fathered and loves."

Tuck nodded. "I can understand that."

"But you still —"

"Yes, I'll see him. I'll tell you when."

On Monday morning, Tuck still was not ready to give Carrie a specific time. He had other things to do, he told her.

"As what?"

"As this morning's surgery. As the choleraesuis case . . ."

"What did the Petri dishes turn up?"

"That our donor was the only one who could have and probably did infect our seven people. And it now develops, as I suspected, that he has a sore on his leg. If it isn't myelitis I'll eat my hat."

"Do you have a hat?"

"Don't tempt me to kiss, or spank you, either, out here in the hall."

"I like you to be tempted. All right. So he has a myelitis. Do you think he knew . . . ?"

"That he was breeding trouble? No, ma'am, I don't. I believe that he can be unaware that he has a serious bone infection. Blood banks don't inquire about such things. But when we treat him for myelitis, I am going to brand him as being unfit to give or sell blood ever again."

"Will that work?"

"Branding his arm might."

"And then you will . . ."

"Good night, Carrie, you *are* a nag, aren't you?"

"When provoked into it, yes, I am."

"Well, it just may pay off. Now will you let me get on to scrub?"

She did let him, and he was glad that she

hadn't "nagged" him into revealing that he was planning to talk to Ortho about Bob's case and the family situation.

But he already had made the appointment to see the head of Orthopedic Surgery at noon. They would eat lunch together, all other factors favorable.

They were. At least favorable enough that he could talk to his Chief, whom he liked and had trusted since he first had chosen orthopedics for his specialty and had acquired Dr. Humphrey as his advisor. Things had changed a bit in fifteen years. Humphrey's hair now was snow-white. Tuck had narrowed his medical field to bone diseases, but also the two were now colleagues and friends on a somewhat equal level. One was Chief of the Service on which Tuck was a valued Staff. The change was not important. Tuck could talk to Bob Humphrey with complete confidence in whatever advice might be forthcoming.

Enjoying their chops and avocado salad, Tuck let Dr. Humphrey congratulate him on the cholerae-suis detection. "That sort of thing does our hospital no harm," said the older man.

"I enjoy detective work. And compared with the problem I am bringing to you today, it was pie."

"It was, eh?"

"I think so, sir. Because, you see, there is this child . . ."

And he told about Bob. He identified Megan, whom Dr. Humphrey remembered, and would have expanded upon that memory. Then Tuck identified Carrie. "I am going to marry her, sir."

"She's an excellent o.r. head. And a pretty girl besides."

"You do know Carrie," Tuck said. "Well, this child . . ."

And he quickly outlined the situation. The boy surely needed help, he said, "and as quickly as possible."

"You suspect . . ."

"A myeloma, yes, sir, I do."

"Then get at it, Tuck."

"That's not so easy. I don't know how to get to the father, or around him."

"What's wrong with the man? Can't you talk to him?"

"I don't believe he will give me the chance, sir."

"He's frightened."

"I am sure he is. He also may think that if he stays blind to the frightening trouble, it will go away."

"Has this child seen any doctor?"

"I am sure he has not. Not for the leg

problem. Megan and Carrie want me to admit him on Megan's signature."

"Well, you could, of course, but that's like laying snake eggs in the dove's nest."

"I told you I had a problem."

"Well, you do seem to. How about a slab of chocolate pie?"

"Nothing makes me fat, sir."

"Good for you. Well, Tuck, I think Miss Reynolds is the one to approach and work on her sister and the husband. Does she live with them?"

"Oh, no, sir. They live out in Edgewood. Carrie has her own apartment near the hospital. She never did live with the Vashons."

"Smart of both parties. Well, Tuck, you must know it is a terrible thing to have conflict between a man and his wife over a sick child."

"I do know it, sir. But the child . . . Bob is an enchanting little boy. Appealing. Only four."

"You had better consider him more impersonally, son."

"I know that. And I think I would. But, want to or not, personalities do enter the case. However, the basic truth is, he needs help, and soon."

"And quickly," the Chief amended. "I suppose you want me to tell you what to do."

Tuck shook his head. "Not exactly," he said. "But I do want you to understand what I decide to do."

Dr. Humphrey enjoyed a forkful of his pie. "And terrible or not, you feel you must force this conflict between Megan Reynolds and her husband."

"It should not reduce to such terms."

"No, it should not. But in my spot — Would you like to be Ortho Chief, Tucker?"

Tuck laughed. "Not in a thousand years, sir!"

"I thought not. Well, I shall try to be understanding of the situation if this case gets you into trouble."

"I hope it won't, sir. There should be a way . . ."

"There might be. You work on finding that way, remembering, as you will, that time is of the essence."

"I have thought of going straight to the father, away from the women . . ."

"And he, quite rightly, could ask what business his son's leg was to you."

"I could tell him. I feel very strongly about this."

"I can see that you do. And perhaps that is one of your problems."

"How's that?"

"You've been an M.D. for — how long?

Fifteen or twenty years. In that time, haven't you learned that you can't care for all the people in this world?"

Tuck made a gesture of impatience.

"Of course you know that," agreed the Chief. "Now, isn't it time for you to realize that a case of this sort can fill your mind to the point . . . I know you haven't neglected your other cases, Tuck."

But there had been that day, a week ago, when Tuck had done five surgicals in a long, long day, and in that time had also thought about the Vashons, had relived his knowledge of Megan and Carrie, had thought, and thought, about his position in the relationship . . .

"I see what you mean, doctor," he said now, and humbly.

"Good! That is a beginning. Now you can back off a bit and consider your problem as being just that, rather than a chunk of your own flesh being torn from your person."

Tuck sat back and touched his napkin to his lips. "I don't know if it would help if I knew the family better. If Vashon knew me."

"It might. It might not."

"I know the girls, sir. As I said, Carrie and I are going to marry. I've known her since she was fourteen, first through Megan when she worked in the Complex. She used to invite the students and interns out to her home. But of course when she married out of the medical profession, things changed."

"The boy — your patient . . ."

"Bob wasn't born when they first married, sir. They must have waited for five or six years."

"Deliberately?"

"I don't know. I tell you, I have been out of touch."

"If they badly wanted a child, and seemed not able to have one . . ."

"They are tense about the boy. His illness seems a special threat to them. But what the circumstances of his birth were, I don't know."

"And that shouldn't change the fact that the kid has developed a myeloma."

"It doesn't change the medical facts, no, sir. It does not. As I say, I lost touch with the family. The girls' parents died. There were no more Sunday evening gatherings of hungry students and interns. When Carrie wanted to take on nursing, she asked me for a recommendation and help. But she could have got in without me. However . . ."

"Yes. I understand."

"Megan left the hospital when she became pregnant. And so far as I know, even since I've known Carrie, there has been no suggestion that Stowe Vashon has ever been anything but a proper man, and a proper husband."

No need to tell the Chief how Megan had come to marry the young attorney. Besides, he was ready to terminate the discussion.

And before determining that he and Carrie loved each other, Tuck had decided that there was no reason at all to think Vashon had continued his — his — his *what?* His "interest" in his wife's sister.

So —

After a few sentences about letting the Chief know how things were working out, Tuck went up to surgical and looked at the morning's case.

And thought about Bob Vashon. The Chief had given him a well-earned rebuke on that one, though Tuck did not believe he had neglected his other work and interests . . . Take the cholerae-suis case. He had given that one his best attention. Every one of last Monday's marathon-surgery patients was doing well. He —

But of course he had put a lot of thought and agony to Bob's situation. However, it always did upset him for a child to develop symptoms. Even when medical care could be smoothly arranged for the patient, Tuck always did have to tell himself to wait for the tests, wait until he had all the facts.

He should tell himself that now. As things now stood Tuck was only guessing that there was something wrong with Bob's bones. He had not examined the child, no blood had been drawn, certainly there had been no mention of marrow tests or biopsy.

He pointed this out to Carrie when she found a question to ask him in his office.

"But you're experienced with these things, Tuck," she reminded him. "I've known you to make a diagnosis on a child walking ahead of us at the zoo."

Yes, she had. And she had restrained him from approaching the parents to tell them to take their child to a clinic. "You know when a case comes into your office — I believe you are rightly worried about Bob."

He told her about his lunch with Dr. Humphrey.

"In the Staff dinning room?"

"I rate that on my own."

"Of course you do, Tuck, but you usually settle for a quick spaghetti in the personnel caff. What did you have to eat?"

He told her. He told her what the Chief had to say about his preoccupation with one case. "Not just Bob. Any case."

94

"Do you think you could change?"

"I doubt it. He also asked, in a dozen ways, if Megan and Stowe loved their son."

She sat back, shocked and stricken. "But of course they do, Tuck!" she cried.

"They wanted him before he was born?"

"I am sure they did. They both, from the first, have been delighted with the child . . . He was a darling baby, sturdy, wide-eyed. He was born with the personality he has now. And, yes, Stowe loved him. He is not a demonstrative man, you know."

Tuck sat shaking his head.

"Well, he isn't," Carrie said. "But he loved — does love — Bob. And he was literally torn to pieces when Bob first started to fail, to show symptoms —"

"Stumbled," said Tuck.

Carrie smoothed the front of her o.r. gown. "Yes," she said faintly, "and complained that his leg hurt. Then there was the limp which you noticed."

The tall man lifted himself from his chair. "I wish I had taken up farming," he said, his tone anguished.

"Oh, Tuck, I am sorry."

"I won't go so far as to say that I wish I didn't know you or Megan and Bob. But I do resent the fact that I have so much more than the medical facts to consider."

She pushed the office door closed with her foot, and then went to him.

"I love you for caring," she said earnestly, her eyes searching his face. "I love you for wanting to help Bob."

"I'm not getting into this because I love you, Carrie. Though you know I do. But I am — I hope I am ready to help any child who needs my knowledge and skill."

"I know that, Tuck."

"But there is another thing you may not know." He spoke angrily, gruffly. "I also stand ready to fight and defeat stubborn narrow-mindedness when I meet up with it. I hope I can help Bob, with the father agreeing to that help. But, Carrie, I promise you if I can't manage that, I am going to help the kid in any way that I can!"

Her eyes were filled with tears, but she tried to smile. "I want to help him too," she said.

"Don't you think Stowe wants that?"

"Yes. I am sure he does. Only —"

"He is trying to play ostrich. O.K. Now this is what I want you — no, *Megan* — to do. I want her to tell Stowe she is taking Bob to a pediatrician to see why his leg hurts. His regular pediatrician would be best. But, remember, she is to tell her husband."

"I'll tell her that."

"Yes. And then you stay out of it."

"I'll try. But I know what the pediatrician will say."

He frowned. "He'll suggest an orthopod."

"Yes. Of course he will. And that ortho will be you."

He groaned, and Carrie lifted herself to kiss his cheek. "You'll help him, Tuck," she said earnestly.

He tried to smile. "We both hope," he conceded.

And quite soon, before the end of the week, Tuck found on his day's schedule that he had a new patient in the children's ward, a boy named Robert Vashon, entered by a staff pediatrician. Of course the brief memo did not say a thing about the parents and their agreement. But there must have been something, he and Carrie decided.

"Did Megan tell you . . . ?"

"She told me yesterday afternoon, late, that she had taken Bob to the pediatrician."

"With Stowe's consent?"

"Oh, I suppose so."

Tuck's lips thinned.

"And she said the case was being referred to you."

"I'll be hearing from Dr. Stirling."

"Let's go see him." She started down the corridor.

Tuck seized her arm. "Hey, hey!" he cried. "We've gone to some lengths to have this proceed according to proper ethics. Stirling will call me, or come and ask me to accompany him. He'll tell me what he's found, what he suspects . . ."

"And Bob will greet you like a long, lost uncle!"

Tuck laughed. "At least he won't be afraid of me."

"No. He won't. But —"

"Just be patient, will you, Carrie?"

She laughed. A little. "I will if you will," she challenged.

And of course the pediatrician did get in touch. He told Tuck about Bob. "He's developed this quite quickly. I saw him in the early spring, and there was nothing . . ." Would Dr. Fairbairn find time to look at the boy, and consult with Dr. Stirling sometime that afternoon?

Tuck agreed, his tone quiet. And he found a way to tell Carrie of the appointment.

"Have you seen Bob?"

"Not yet. But I am pretty sure you have."

"Oh, yes. He thinks there is too much white being worn in this joint."

"Did he call it that?"

"He certainly did."

"Then I won't wear my new white coat when I gallop down there to see what goes on."

"Can I . . . ?"

"No, you can't," he answered her. "You belong up here on three. Bob's down on two, as you know."

But, shortly, he would be on three. They both knew that. And for a long minute they gazed down along the third floor's shining corridor.

"Well," said Carrie, "since I guess you are just about his favorite uncle. You'll" — her voice trembled — "you will tell me . . ."

He pressed her arm. "I'll tell you," he promised.

He found Bob completely in charge of the small ward where he had been assigned. He did greet Tuck effusively, and asked where his white shoes were.

"Being cleaned," Tuck told him. "Is your mother around?"

"She's around somewhere," said Bob airily. "In here's my new friends. That boy over there is named Morgan. He's nice but I never knew anybody before named Morgan, did you?"

Tuck nodded to the small, wide-eyed boy

99

in the high bed. "Hi-ya, Morgan," he said.

"And that's John, and the other one is Wayne. He's asleep, maybe."

Bob wore a bright blue woolly robe over his pajamas. "Bob's supposed to be in bed too," Morgan volunteered. "He ain't never been in no hospital before."

"Then he has a lot to learn, hasn't he, Morgan?" Tuck commented. "Come along, friend Bob. If you're supposed to be in bed . . ."

Bob agreed, though reluctantly. Did he have to take off his new robe? And what was that tall building way over there? And why did the nurse keep coming in the room? Where did his mother go? Carrie had been to see him. Did Tuck know that? And he didn't like shots. Did Tuck know *that?*

And all the time, his clear voice faded steadily, and his eyes got bigger. Tuck read the chart; he examined the little boy. He let Bob listen to his own heart, and then to Tuck's.

"Wheeee! You do thump!" said the little boy.

So Morgan and John wanted to listen too.

And Megan came in, her eyes fearful. Tuck drew her into the hall. "Try not to scare the pants off the boy!" he told her roughly.

"But I am scared, Tuck!"

"I know, but . . ."

"All these things are hard, Megan. I knew that before I ever specialized."

And then there were the tests, some of which bewildered, some frightened the little boy. There were the consultations of doctors around the crib bed, and again in Tuck Fairbairn's office. Bob was moved up to three, and the surgeon was ready to tell the family about the child.

Carrie had been reading the charts. And Tuck, knowing that she did, had said nothing. Except to tell her not to let Megan know that she was doing it. "She'll expect you to come up with a firsthand general diagnosis."

"I'm sorry we had to get you into this, Tuck," she said, her face showing her sorrow.

"It's my job."

"Not for a family member. Not for someone you love."

"Oh, yes, it is. Though of course sometimes I can't *do* anything for the member."

She searched his face. "Can you do anything for Bob?" she asked.

"I sincerely hope someone can."

"I'd not be satisfied with anyone else."

★ ★ ★

Much too soon, as quickly as possible, the day came, the hour, the minute, when the family must be told of the doctors' decision, of the diagnosis.

Dr. Fairbairn was present, Dr. Moore, Dr. Humphrey, and Dr. Stirling the pediatrician. Megan and Carrie sat side by side on a small couch, holding each other's hand, trying to appear quiet, and ready. Megan wore a blue suit with a red scarf tucked into the throat of it, the points of it up against her cheek which, under the makeup, was stone-white. Carrie was apparently calm; she wore a white blouse, its collar crisp against a rose-colored sweater and cardigan.

When the four doctors came in, Dr. Fairbairn cast a quick glance around the small room. "Where is Stowe?" he asked.

The women exchanged glances. "He — won't be able to make it," said Megan, almost in a whisper.

"He won't come," said Carrie, more forcefully. "He is afraid of what you will tell us."

Everyone there was thinking of the little redheaded boy manfully wearing his blue robe, his fate in the hands of these people.

"Bob's father should be here," said Tuck sternly.

Megan glanced at the other men. "My husband," she said, "dislikes medical things. He . . ."

"We get people like that all the time," said Dr. Humphrey. "But when a man has a son, he should learn to face certain unpleasant circumstances."

"I know that, Dr. Humphrey," said Megan, her voice stronger. "But — can't you consider me a member of Bob's family?"

"I suppose we'll have to do that, Megan. Tucker?"

All eyes turned to the tall, dark man who stood in the corner of the room. Carrie wanted to go to him, to let her touch give him such strength as was possible.

She sat still, and watched him shift the papers in his hand.

"You each would understand the medical terms," he said crisply. "We have made every test in the book. We have explored every possibility. But I think in this situation a short verdict would be best. We have found that Bob has cancer of the bone; I can show you the x-rays. The bone looks like moth-eaten tissue. This is an extremely rare type of a disease which is extremely rare in children. The name is Ewing's sarcoma." He glanced at Carrie. She closed her eyes for a second.

Megan sobbed.

"And after amputation, which is imperative, we shall try radiation and chemotherapy to detect, and possibly delay, or correct its spread to other parts of the body. But he must lose the leg, and as soon as possible. We must immediately attend to that."

"Does he know?"

"Not yet. We would like his parents to tell him."

"Stowe won't," said Megan. "He won't admit such a thing to himself. He will never consent to amputation."

"Well, he'll have to do that too!" Tuck was angry, and sounded that way.

Megan sat with her fingers pressed to her mouth. She wore red gloves and they showed up vividly against her white face. "Tuck . . . ?" she asked pitiably.

He went swiftly to her. Carrie moved so that he could sit beside her, take her hands in his and try to comfort her. But there was no way of comforting her. Yes, she agreed, Bob was only a little boy. Still a baby, in many ways.

"But he — I think he may take this better than any of us older people could or would. He —"

"But he doesn't *know!*" cried Megan. "He is too young to look ahead and realize what it will mean for him to go through life with only one leg! How are you going to *tell* him a thing like that?"

Her voice lifted shrilly. Carrie went to her other side and tried to hush her. She must calm down, she said, she must get control of herself. She could not face Bob while in this hysterical mood. She and Stowe . . .

At this, Megan sprang to her feet. *"Me and Stowe!"* she cried. "How can I tell *him?* He didn't want Bob brought here to the hospital. He certainly won't let me or anyone tell him that his son — Oh, Carrie, Carrie, what *are* we going to do?"

The doctors, except Tuck, had left the room, departing quietly. They knew that this particular scene had to be gone through. Fairbairn had gone through variations on it many times before. He would handle it.

Only — this time — he could not seem to handle it. Megan was beyond all reason. She wept and talked wildly of Bob, of his precious blue robe. How could anyone tell that child . . . ? Well, if the operation had to take place, couldn't they just *do* it? This past week they had trundled the baby off for x-rays and biopsies . . . Shouldn't they just — ?

Tuck waited her out. Carrie did. Then the doctor mentioned the trust which the boy's parents had instilled in him.

"Trust in *you*." cried Megan accusingly.

"Yes, in me. He has let me make all the tests, trusting me, listening to my explanations."

"I wish you would have worked a little on Stowe," said Megan grimly. "He thinks you are a monster."

"He thinks all doctors are monsters," said Carrie softly. "He cannot understand a man's going into such a profession."

Tuck nodded, and rubbed his thick, dark hair back from his face. "Why don't we . . . ?" he asked, and certainly the idea was not a new one. "Why don't we hand Bob's case over to another hospital? Another man? We could move him to Peter Brent, to Mayo's . . ."

Carrie joggled his arm. "You know they aren't better hospitals, Tuck," she said firmly.

"But if Stowe Vashon has a feeling against me personally —"

"He doesn't. How could he, Tuck? He hardly knows you. He admits that he doesn't know you. I told him that he did know you when you used to come to our house for Sunday supper, but he says he cannot place you."

"We can believe that. I feel that I don't know him. But I've 'not known' hundreds of fathers, and yet they stand ready to listen to me."

"We have two choices, Carrie," he said finally. "One of them is immediate surgery."

"I know it," she conceded helplessly.

"That surgery is the only chance we can give the boy for life. The second choice is to stand back and watch the cancer spread, eventually reach a vital organ, and then Stowe can watch him die."

"You're being blunt, Tuck."

"I can't find any prettier picture to paint, Carrie. And while I am willing to tell Vashon myself, wherever I can find him, I would much rather you girls would tell him, just as we have discussed it today. Bob has one chance in a hundred. Surgery will give him that chance. So get with it, ladies. Go tell Megan's husband what the odds are."

"He won't listen to surgery," said Megan, stripping off her red gloves. "May I go to see Bob?"

"Not in this mood, I think, dear. I'll take you down to your car. And I shall expect to hear from you by this time tomorrow."

"In a way," said Megan, "you're as stubborn as Stowe is."

"Then Carrie should know how to handle him."

★ ★ ★

Tuck saw them on their way, supposing that they would discuss ways and means to convince Stowe. What a guy he must be. Before this, the doctor had met up with families whose religion ruled out surgery; he had met up with discouragement and fear. Despondency. But prejudice — blind refusal to face facts . . .

He went to the desk to consult his day's schedule. "What's the joke for the day, doctor?" asked the floor nurse.

Tuck stared at her blankly. "A joke for *today?*" he asked, as if he had never known such a thing.

The nurse watched him go down the corridor. "He's got it bad about something," she told the intern who was behind her, seated at the chart desk.

"It's a member of Carrie Reynolds' family," the intern explained. "An amputation. And the whole kith and kin are against it."

"He'll do it anyway."

"How can he? There are consent papers."

"He'll do it."

Four

In his own office, Stowe Vashon was called "old stone face." This was not entirely a criticism. His associates simply knew that his feelings almost never showed themselves. He was a clever, resourceful attorney. He knew pain, he knew anger, and he knew concern. But he had schooled himself not to show any emotion in his face. He was a tall man, always conservatively dressed. He still wore his red-blond hair in a thick crew cut, perhaps a little longer than had been the style current ten years ago. He spoke quietly, but always to the point. His secretary insisted that she liked him.

At home, he was not a great deal different from the attorney in his wood-paneled office, or before a judge in the courtroom. He lived in an attractive, modern, three-bedroom home in the prosperous suburb of Edgewood. He had a good-looking wife, and a little boy whom he adored. On that subject, his eyes could shine, his voice quicken. The office knew that Mr. Vashon's boy was in the hospital. "Something wrong with his leg; he doesn't want to talk about it."

Stowe did not want to talk about it either when he came home that late afternoon and put his brief case on the table, hung his coat in the closet, and went into the living room where a fire burned in the stone fireplace, and Carrie and Megan sat together on the couch.

"Carrie," he acknowledged her presence. He bent over to kiss Megan's cheek. "Would you like a drink?"

"No, thank you, Stowe," said Carrie, keeping her voice steady. "I am here —"

"We have something to tell you," Megan took over.

He glanced around from where he had been standing to put two ice cubes into a small, squat glass. "Something wrong?" he asked.

Megan rose and went to him. She still wore the dark blue suit, and the red scarf tied around her throat. "Very wrong, I'm afraid, Stowe," she said softly.

He looked at her closely. "You've been crying."

"All day," she agreed. "I —"

"Can't the bad news wait?" he asked,

carefully putting the cover back on the ice bucket.

"It can't wait at all. And I want Carrie here. She can explain things to you."

Stowe looked at the glass in his hand, then set it down. "Has something happened to Bob?" he asked.

"Something has been happening to him for several months!" cried Megan, her voice rising.

"Don't get hysterical, Megan. It won't help."

"It helps me," she assured him. "When I know, and have to tell you . . ."

Stowe looked beyond her to Carrie. "What's happened to Bob?" he asked.

Carrie stood up. "We were given the doctors' reports today," she said quietly. Her face was dead white, her eyes enormous. "We — The doctors say he has a rare, serious form of cancer."

"And he must lose his leg!" screamed Megan. "Our little boy — one leg — Are you *listening,* Stowe?"

He was listening. His lips had drawn into a straight line. He stepped backward, picked up the glass, and drained it. "I shan't ever permit it," he said firmly.

"I don't think you have any choice," said Carrie, just as firmly.

He stared at her. "Will you please leave me and Megan alone?" he asked coldly.

"No," she said, "I won't. I think you both need me here."

"We don't," he said flatly. "Not unless you mean to listen to what I have to say. You two women are hospital-oriented. You think a hospital, a pill, a test, and surgery will solve everything that happens in the world. Yours is a ghoulish profession, Carrie. Megan's was almost as bad. My *God* . . ."

He went across to the windows and stood staring out at the darkening landscape, the lawn, the road that swept up and around before the other attractive houses in this subdivision. Two boys went by on bicycles. A car went along the street.

"I reluctantly let Megan take Bob to the hospital," he said, without turning, "because the boy seemed to have bruised his leg. Once there, of course, you medical people hunted for and found all sorts of things wrong with him." He turned and faced them accusingly. "Where in hell could he get cancer?" he demanded.

"If doctors could answer that question," said Carrie, her voice as brittle as thin ice, "their worst problems would be over."

"Yet they know cancer when they see it," Stowe countered.

"Of course they do. It is quite plainly defined on slides under a microscope. Stowe, I don't think you should argue *that* point just now."

"I'll argue every damn thing I can to save my boy."

"I can understand . . ."

"How can you understand? Megan does not."

"Oh, yes, she does, Stowe. And now, when you should be comforting her, strengthening her —"

"Is this verdict final?" asked the attorney. "Aren't there other hospitals, other doctors who might venture to disagree with your precious Dr. Fairbairn?"

Carrie put a warning hand out to silence Megan. Stowe was frightened. His hatefulness was his first way to combat that fear. "There were other doctors," she said quietly. And she listed the names. "You were asked to be present when they made their reports this morning."

"And they all said," cried Megan, "that the only way to save Bob's life was to . . ."

"You mean, your friend Tuck says that. You two females are hospital obsessed. You can't see any other way to solve a problem. Bob bruised his leg, he limped, you put him in the hospital, and the great and wonderful

Tucker Fairbairn says the leg must come off. For a *bruise!* Nobody gives any thought to what this will mean to the boy. What it will mean to *you*, Megan!"

"And to you," said his wife, now quiet, determined.

"Because it's *you* whom you are thinking of, Stowe. *You* are afraid. *You* can't face what this will mean. You would rather have a dead son than a crippled one. You —"

"Hush, Megan," said Carrie, going to her. "Of course Stowe is frightened, of course he is shocked. Give him time. Let him talk to Tuck. He should have done so long before this. He knows he must do it now."

Stowe swung on her, and for a moment even he thought he would strike the woman. "I wish you would leave," he said tightly. "Because this is none of your business."

"I dearly love Bob."

"You —" Then his voice broke, his control. "You have no idea," he cried, "how *I* love that boy!"

"Then," said Carrie, "do what you can to save his life. Let Tuck explain to you . . ."

"If I ever see the guy," cried Stowe, "I'll kill him. I promise you both that I will."

"But Tuck isn't to blame for what has

114

happened to Bob," cried Megan. "He is a very good surgeon, he knows about bone diseases. But he himself would agree if you decided you want another doctor, or if you wanted to take him to Mayo's, or Chicago, or to Barnes in St. Louis. He wouldn't be — He would *want* you to feel that Bob was getting the very best care possible. Oh, please, Stowe! Please just talk to him."

It was no use. Stowe had set his stubborn mind and will against this awful thing.

"And it is awful," Megan reminded Carrie.

"I believe Tuck knows that better than any of us, Megan."

"Perhaps if Tuck would come here . . ."

"He might. But I think Stowe must be the one to go to him."

Tuck Fairbairn was not a conceited man. But he had worked his way through all the mazes which led to his present position as a top-notch surgeon and diagnostician. He had met up with families who were stunned with the diagnoses which he sometimes had to give; he had known those who took the patient elsewhere. He had never before been asked to operate against the will and the agreement of a child's father.

He said, yes, he would talk to Stowe

Vashon. It should be soon. All right, Stowe wouldn't talk to him. He would "kill" the surgeon who operated without his agreement. "I shall not give him that chance, Carrie," he told the young woman. "Let Moore or even Humphrey do it. We can bring a man in from outside — just so it gets done, and soon."

"You are being reasonable," said Carrie.

"And Stowe is not."

"No, he is not. I never saw a man act as he is doing."

"They do, sometimes. Usually from religious convictions."

"Stowe is just being stubborn."

"And I am being knife-happy."

"Oh, Tuck, darling . . ."

He smiled at her. "How is Megan taking this?"

"She is pitiful. She is torn into shreds by her love for Bob, her horror at the thought of amputation, and bewilderment that nothing, literally nothing, will move Stowe."

"I could do a little killing myself there," said Tuck grimly.

It was the year's first really cold day; occasional snow flurries blew in with the gale winds from the lake and the cold lands north of the city. But, to get free of the hospital, hoping to clear their minds of all the arguing, the persuading, Tuck and Carrie had bundled into warm coats, tugged knitted caps down over their ears, thrust their gloved hands deep into the pockets of their coats, and were "taking a walk."

They met few people afoot; the waters of the lake were iron-gray, frothed with the spume which sometimes touched their cheeks. Their own breath showed white vapor. But they would walk a certain distance, turn and come back to the door of Carrie's apartment, go upstairs, and —

"If I kissed you now," said Tuck, "it would take a blowtorch to get us apart."

". . . might be worth it . . ." said Carrie, the words blown away from them.

He put his hand through her arm, he held her close, and turned. Their walk had been long enough. The lights on the cars and in the tall buildings were getting more brilliantly red. They no longer tried to talk. Just to be close was enough.

The doorman agreed that he thought they were crazy. "You being doctors and all," he said reprovingly.

"Is it going to snow, Benjy?" Tuck asked him, pulling his cap from his head.

"It already do snow, doctor. Ain't you notice?"

Tuck and Carrie laughed, and went into the elevator. Their frigid walk had done its work. Now they could brew coffee, sit and talk about the problem which in no way had been diminished, but which could be considered by itself.

"I wish we were out at your place," said Carrie, busy with the coffee pot. "We could have an open fire . . ."

"Your car's downstairs, mine is at the hospital — we could make it in an hour."

"And get snowed in."

"Let's go!" said Tuck enthusiastically.

Carrie laughed. He would do it with one word of encouragement.

"I really like your place," said Tuck, as if reassuring himself. Carrie's was in an older apartment house; hers was a corner unit, with windows on three sides of the living room. She had filled them with plants, tall ones in tubs on the floor, others hanging before the glass. There was a round oak table, with rush-bottomed chairs pulled up to it, a bowl of fruit hospitably inviting. There was a rocking chair, and a low couch of brown velvet. In the next room, her bed was covered with a patchwork quilt.

Tuck felt completely at home here, and helped prepare a meal of broiled chops, a can of corn thickened with egg and quickly turned into a custard. There were hot rolls, honey, and the big pot of coffee.

"Domesticated is the word for Fairbairn," said Tuck when they sat down to the meal.

"I like it among all the other names," said Carrie.

"That means I'll have to wash the dishes," he predicted. "But together we are pretty good cooks."

"Yes, and I didn't think I would be able to eat a bite," she said, her face saddening. "Oh, Tuck, what are we going to do?"

"We should have made a salad," he answered.

"There's fresh fruit. But I can't keep Bob off my mind."

"I know. We'll talk about it."

She nibbled at her chop bone and studied the man's face. Tuck was a big man, with broad shoulders, powerful arms, and a strong face which she thought handsome because of its strength. His hair was thick and black, and could be brushed into submission but usually it was ruffed as by the knitted cap which he had worn this evening, or the cap which he wore in the hospital o.r. and pushed from his head without regard for appearances.

"What are you thinking about?" he asked now, taking another roll. "Besides . . ."

"I know the besides. I was thinking about how long we had known each other, and how long it took us to find out that we loved each other."

"I think we knew it all along," he said.

"Did we?" she asked, her blue eyes wide with surprise. "Then —"

"These things have to ripen," he instructed her. "When I first knew you, I was showing you how to braid your hair."

"I've often wondered. Where did you learn to do that?"

"My sister had a little girl. She wanted her to wear braids but she made an unholy mess of braiding the stuff. So, from a book she had, I figured out the way to do it."

"Your surgeon's fingers."

"Could be. And then of course I couldn't ask a kid in braids to marry me. For years and years I hadn't a thin dime in my pocket."

"I could have decided to marry some other guy."

"I thought of that. But, those days, I was taking all sorts of risks. And studying, and never sleeping, and I didn't have a bed of my own, let alone one I could ask you to share. But I will say this: I knew I loved you before we spent that night in front of my fire at home."

120

"We did not spend the night!" Her cheeks were bright red.

"We could have."

Yes, they could have. "Soon . . ." said Carrie softly, reaching her hand to his.

"I'm not a guy to go 'round saying, 'I love you,' every fifteen minutes, by the coo-coo clock."

"You don't need to be. I'll know. We knew last spring, and as soon as we get Bob taken care of . . ."

He stood up. He set two pears on the table top. He carried everything else to the tiny kitchen, scraped the dishes, put things into the washer, scoured the broiler and wiped everything shining clean. "You know," he said, "I'll never wash the dishes after we are married."

She gazed at him thoughtfully. "Then maybe the whole deal just might fall through."

She was teasing, but such a look of alarm stilled Tuck's face that she went to him quickly. "Oh, Tuck, darling!" she cried. She put her arms about him and kissed him. She felt his sigh, and she kissed him again. "You need not ever wash the broiler again!" she whispered in his ear.

He laughed and crushed her so closely in his embrace that she protested.

"If we were younger," he said, "I would not go out in that weather again tonight."

"We're young enough."

"But old enough too. At least, I am. I want things right between us, Carrie. Really right."

She nodded. "I'm that old too," she confessed.

He kissed her again. "Now!" he said, "we'll eat our pears and talk. You will tell me again exactly what you and Megan and Stowe said this afternoon. He comes to the hospital to see the kid, you know."

"Yes. When he knows he won't run into you."

"Just what does he have against me?"

"You're the surgeon who thinks Bob —"

He piled cushions into the corner of the couch. "Correction," he said. "Who *knows* Bob has to have that surgery."

She sat down in the nest which he had made. She kicked off her shoes, and accepted the pear. It was a beautiful one, with a red cheek. She held it in her hands, and watched him take a knife and precisely cut the other pear into thin strips which he alternately ate and fed to her. And she told him each word that had been said that afternoon in the Vashon living room.

"Why didn't he get the report himself at

the hospital?" Tuck asked, of himself rather than Carrie.

"For the same reason he said so positively that he would not permit you to operate."

"He can let Moore do it, take the boy to Chicago, or Rochester. The doctors there would accept our findings, and operate. It has to be done, Carrie."

"I know that," she said, "and Megan knows it. Though this tears her to pieces, Tuck."

"I know. I've seen her fondling Bob's little hand, and even his bare foot. And if the truth is known — I am not supposed to get personal about a patient, Carrie. And usually I don't. But, *gee, pops,* girl . . ."

She moved enough to kiss his cheek. He wiped his knife blade and put it away, then wiped his hands and her lips with the napkin. She still held the second pear.

"What . . . ?" he began, coughed, and tried a second time. "What happens now?"

She shook her head, her fine, soft hair clinging to his sweater.

"I cannot operate without the parents' consent."

"Megan knows that."

"And Stowe is counting on it. Because he knows it too."

He put his hands on her cheeks and set

her head against a square velvet pillow. Then he leaned toward her and kissed her lips. "I have to get back to the hospital," he said. "Rounds, and that post-op."

She stood up. "I'll go with you," she said. She knew all about the post-op. Another child, a boy only a year older than Bob.

"It's snowing," Tuck told her.

"So it's snowing. I'll drive you there. We'll make rounds and you can pick up your car, follow me back here . . ."

He didn't argue. Snow didn't make that much of a hazard this early in the season. It was still early in the evening, and in their part of the country — Besides, it was a comfort to be together.

While she changed into a uniform, as she had to do to make rounds with the surgeon, he went to the bookshelves which rounded one corner of the room. They filled the space from floor to ceiling and held literally everything from *The Wind in the Willows* to Toynbee. When she came out of the bedroom, Carrie stood for a minute watching him. What a guy Tuck Fairbairn was. Something like the pear which she had put back into the bowl. Handsome, firm, and sweet at heart.

"Let's go," she said softly. He turned and smiled at her. "I like you in white," he assured her.

★ ★ ★

The hospital — Skull and Bones — was lighted from its wide, canopied front door to the glass-windowed penthouse on the roof. As were all the buildings of the Complex. The snow still blew about, stinging one's face, but only drifting into small heaps against a curbing, or blowing like mist along a driveway.

"We won't make ten inches by morning," Tuck told Carrie as he parked her car.

She laughed. "We can't have everything," she reminded him.

They went upstairs, they checked in, Carrie in her hooded blue cape, the doctor still in his corduroys and heavy short coat. "Where did you two come from?" the floor nurse asked them.

"You'd be surprised . . ." said Carrie.

"Dinner together?" the nurse asked her, watching Tuck go down the hall for a white jacket or lab coat.

"We took a walk," said Carrie. "He's worried about the Vashon boy."

"Who isn't? He still is not scheduled."

"I know. I am going to make rounds with Dr. Fairbairn."

"I figured that was the idea. He's in a sad business."

"Someone has to do it. When he cures a

patient, it's a perfectly wonderful business."

"Yes, it is. Do you think Bob Vashon . . . ?"

"I'm not paid to think. But I am sure Tuck is hopeful."

"Then I'll be hopeful too. Bob is such a dear little boy. Oh and, Carrie, be sure to take him to thirty-six, will you? That's another boy who needs him."

Tuck was coming toward them, changed completely into white shoes, trousers, and jacket. "I thought I'd give you girls a treat," he said, going around to the chart desk.

"Do you want the intern, doctor?" asked the floor nurse.

"If he's not busy . . ."

"Who ever heard of an intern being busy?" asked the nurse, pressing a button.

They made the rounds of the surgical beds. Bob Vashon greeted them happily. He was thinner than he had been when he'd entered a week ago, and his manner had become just a little wary. Now, he was obediently staying in bed. "That's my Aunt Carrie," he told the other children on the ward. "The big doctor is named Tuck, and I can call him that."

"Everybody calls him that," said Carrie, pulling down the shirt of Bob's pajamas.

"No, sir, they don't," said Bob. "The

doctors and nurses call him 'doctor.' They say, 'Yes, doctor, no doctor.' "

"And that doctor'll get you if you're too sassy," Tuck assured him. "How's the old leg feel?"

"All right, when you don't pinch it and do stunts."

"Then we won't do any stunts tonight. How about going to sleep?"

"Not before the lights go out."

"Is that the way they do things around here?"

"They do all sorts of crazy things."

"I'll bet they do. Where's Mike?"

"Oh, he got op'rated this morning. They put him in a private room for that."

"Away from all you noisy talkative guys. I see. Well, I'll have to hunt for him, won't I?"

"He's in thirty-six," said the intern. "And not . . ."

"Then we'll mush right down to thirty-six," said Tuck quickly and loudly. "Good night, kids. See you tomorrow."

In the corridor, the intern said, "I'm sorry, sir."

Tuck nodded Carrie smiled at the young doctor. "Old or young," she reminded him, "we don't give reports on one patient to another."

"I know that, Miss Reynolds. I really do

know it. When is Bob going to have his surgery?"

She only nodded to him, and hurried after Dr. Fairbairn. "Yes, doctor, no, doctor," he was muttering.

It was almost bedtime, and the corridor was busy with departing visitors, nurses hurrying about their duties, a child crying desolately because his mother had left him.

"Bob has had good spirits," said Carrie, as if reassuring herself.

"And that does help," said the intern.

Mike, in thirty-six, was a very small boy in a very white, very big bed. An aide sat beside him, holding the i.v. tube in place. Mike had had a shoulder injury six months before; it had not been cared for, and Tuck had had to scrape infected bone tissues and graft new . . .

"His father is coming in at midnight," said the aide. "His mother has children at home."

Tuck read the chart; he bent over the bed. Mike did not want to talk. Yes, his arm hurt . . . He spoke in a whisper, and gasped at each word.

"ICU?" asked the intern.

"We may have to move him," Tucker agreed. "His lungs aren't doing their job.

For now I suggest oxygen by nasal canula and we had better continue the intravenous feeding."

"That means a Special," said Carrie.

Tuck glanced at her. "Yes," he agreed, "it could."

"Could I?"

Tuck shook his head.

"Please?"

Tuck wrote on the chart, he talked to the intern, then he steered Carrie out of the room.

"He's pitiful, Tuck," she said. "And so frightened. That's his worst problem. I could stay tonight —"

He took her elbow and led her to a space between a Gurney and a fire extinguisher. "Put a NO SMOKING sign on thirty-six," he called loudly to the intern. Then he stepped close to Carrie, shutting her away from the busy hall. "Now you listen to me, my girl," he said. "You cannot Special on Mike tonight. I am letting his father come in after his work shift; Mike will settle down. I'll detail at least two floor personnel to stay with the boy, or I'll send him back to Intensive. But *you* are an o.r. nurse. *You* have a full schedule for tomorrow. Where *you* are needed."

"But —"

"I think we will handle Mike. He's undernourished, but he'll make it, I think. And I am not going to let you agonize over him. You are transferring Bob to this child . . ."

He spoke roughly and sternly. He was the surgeon only, no longer the lover, the gentleman —

"In this hospital," he continued, "we each are trained to do our own job. That aide can monitor the i.v., the intern can set up the canula. Mike's father can comfort Mike. And there is a resident to supervise the whole thing. While you — you've a job to do in o.r. that none of those people could do. So snap out of it, will you, Carrie, and don't give me something else to worry about!"

She looked up at him, her blue eyes wide and dark with amazement. "You're scolding me," she said in wonder. "You —"

He put his two hands on her shoulders. "It sounds that way," he agreed. "But what I am really doing is to affirm myself. I too want to take full care of Mike, to shield him, and help him. I want to wrap Bob up in my heavy coat and run off somewhere with him, and take the entire care of *him!* But that sort of care is not what the children need, Carrie. And do stop looking at me like a hurt child, yourself! You know as well as I do that big hospitals are built and equipped and staffed for the most efficient care possible. You and I — we're just a part of the machine. If we do our part well —"

She rubbed the back of her hand across her eyes. "I'm sorry," she whispered.

He managed a faint smile. "If the pool has a Special, and Mike needs one, he'll have one," he said. "What happened to our intern?"

"I suppose he is doing the canula."

"All right. Let's get on with the rounds, and — I'm sorry I blew my top, Carrie."

"I am sorry you had to."

"O.K. So let's get to work. You say yes, doctor, no, doctor to me, and so far as I am able, I'll keep my yap shut."

They did complete the rounds, more or less in that fashion. Children, adult males, adult females — and back to the children again. When they looked in on Bob, they found him asleep, his precious blue robe cuddled in his arms. "He'll insist on taking that to o.r.," Carrie whispered.

"I hope he gets the chance," grumbled Tuck. "Wait for me?"

"Sure. I'll get us some cocoa."

"You stay right here at this desk and read off what I told you to write on these orders."

"Yes, doctor," she said meekly.

He sat down, then turned the chair so that he faced her and the floor nurse, who pretended to be busy at the other end of the counter. "What finishes me," said Dr. Fairbairn, "is that we have a kid, a little redheaded boy who wants to live, and a redheaded father who is not ready to let him do it."

"Stowe wants desperately for Bob to live," said Carrie earnestly.

Tuck uncapped his pen. "Then he had better get at it, Carrie," he said fiercely. "He had *better.*"

A half hour later they were going down to the garage to pick up their cars. "What?" Carrie asked. "Tuck, what are you going to *do?* About Bob, I mean."

"I am going to see Megan."

"Tonight?"

"No. It's too late. I'll see her tomorrow, after o.r."

"She'll be here; she comes every day, sometimes as often as three times a day."

"I know she does. But I want to talk to her at home. Away from all the yes, doctor, no, doctor protocol. She has worked here; that stuff gets in her way."

"What if Stowe is there?"

"Then I'll talk to him too."

"Would you fight him?"

"Fight him with my fists? Don't worry. No, I wouldn't fight that way with him. But I shall certainly have plenty to say if he is there."

Five

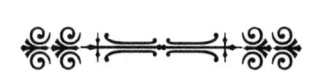

Carrie wanted to go with Tuck. She knew that she should not. She knew that he would refuse to let her. If this was to be his last try — and it could be! Bob needed surgery very soon. And whatever Tuck would find to say to Megan — or to Stowe . . .

She saw him that morning; she saw him come into the hospital, dressed formally, for him, in a sports jacket, and white turtleneck sweater. She saw him in o.r. green, working with concentration. She heard him tell his joke for the day. It was one about the personnel director of a large business firm.

"Our Complex?" asked the Nursing Supe.

"Could be," said Tuck. "Could be any one of the personnel directors who has to fill in these dad-blasted questionaires the government passes out. This one asked, 'How many employees do you have, broken down by sex?' "

At the long desk, everyone waited. The

Supe, the floor nurse, the resident, an anaesthetist studying the o.r. schedule. Carrie.

Tuck nodded. His smile, that day, was a little grim. "This fellow wrote back," he said. " 'Liquor is more of a problem with us.' "

They all laughed. It was one of Tuck's better jokes. Carrie was to hear this one repeated several times that day, and each time she always saw Tuck, his mouth corners turned up in a smile. His thick black lashes hiding most of the worry in his eyes. She *wanted* to be with him. She saw where he had signed out at 2 P.M. Megan's telephone number told where he had gone. She tried to imagine . . .

The Vashon home was in Edgewood, an exclusive suburb of the city where the homes were attractive, though not spectacular. They sat well-spaced, and the Vashon house was approached by a sweeping curve of driveway which ended within a sheltered car port, and a flat front door painted orange. The house itself was of vertical siding painted a very pale green; the upper floor was of the Mansard type with gray, weathered, hand-hewn shingles. It was an attractive home; the long windows spelled hospitality as did the fire on the stone hearth of the living room.

Megan welcomed Tuck quietly, almost formally. "Carrie told me that you were coming," she said.

"I knew she would. Otherwise I would have called."

He crossed over to the fire, as if to warm his hands, which were not cold. The snow of the night before had completely disappeared.

"Your home is attractive," he said. There was a framed crayon portrait of Bob hung on a flat wall, the only picture in the living room.

Megan gestured to the couch. It faced the long double windows and the view of lawn, shrubbery, and trees, with glimpses of other homes — a chimney, the corner of a roof . . .

Tucker sat down, seeing not this pleasant suburban scene or the home of a successful young professional, but his lake on a hot summer day, two splashing, snorting horses ridden by two laughing young women, one of them clutching a little boy wearing a hat too big for his red head.

"I've never taken the chance," said Megan nervously, "of telling you that I am glad you and Carrie are going to be married. I think you are well suited to each other."

She had sat down on a hassock, facing Tuck. Tuck said something about not being sure she was paying him and Carrie a compliment.

"Oh, but I am!" Megan cried. "You are my two very favorite people. And I envy both of you!"

Tuck frowned a little. By accident, or design, Megan sat with the light behind her. He tipped his head to read her dark eyes.

"I can't imagine," she was chattering, "why you don't get about it, now that you have decided. What on earth are you waiting for?"

"For a honeymoon," said Tuck gravely. "For time to have one."

She nodded, and sighed. "You came to talk about Bob," she said then, discarding all attempt at social conversation.

"Yes," said Tuck, "I did. And about you. But mainly, my dear, I wanted to talk to you about the boy's father."

"Stowe."

"Yes. Stowe. Do you realize, Megan, that I don't know the man?"

"He has been avoiding you."

"Since Bob's been my patient. Yes, he has. But before then. I've known you. I have set up a true relationship with your sister. But I have not known your husband. I know, second hand, of his position on surgery for Bob. But he won't discuss the situation with me, nor, so far as I know, with any one of the other doctors. You tell us he won't consent, which means that he must talk to you. So I want to know how you read Stowe Vashon and help me read the man too. You must understand what lies behind the position he has taken. And I want you to make me understand it. Then perhaps I could —"

Her lifted hand silenced him. "I can't read Stowe either, Tuck," she said quietly.

He stared at her. He got to his feet and walked to the window, and came back to stand above her. "I don't understand what you mean," he said. He truly was puzzled. "You're married to the man."

She hugged her knees with her arms and looked up at him. "Sit down," she said, "and I'll try to make you understand."

Still watching her anxiously, he went back to the couch, his right hand smoothing the quilted fabric of its arm. "Megan?" he prompted her.

"Yes," she agreed. "I am going to tell you why I can't read my husband. I want to tell it quickly, but I want to get things straight, so that you will understand."

"I hope," he said gravely.

"I meant, so that you would understand what I am trying to say, Tuck."

So he waited. When she began to speak, it was slowly, as if the words hurt to shape themselves on her lips. "We've been married for about ten years," she said. "Stowe and I. You know that. And after ten years, most wives can read their husbands, can't they?"

"I suppose most of them can. Yes."

"Well, they must be the ones, the wives — What I am saying is that Stowe and I could read each other too, if we ever had loved each other. Now, if we had that love . . ." She fished in the pocket of her red slacks for a Kleenex.

Tuck leaned toward her. "Don't you?" he asked.

She shook her head. "No," she said. "We don't. Not the way married people love, not the way you and Carrie love each other. You don't even need to *read* her. You know what she is thinking and feeling, and she is the same about you. I've watched you this summer . . ."

He sat back. She was right. He and Carrie did know. "Oh, Megan," he said sadly.

She nodded. "Yes," she said. "But we — Oh, at first there was some passion, Tuck. I don't know if you remember how Stowe

139

and I got together in the first place . . ."

Don Moore had told him. "I know you helped him with some lawsuit," he said.

"Yes, I did, and he was grateful. He's stayed grateful for that. At the time, well, he was up in the clouds. I have never seen him so excited before or since. And out of gratitude, he took me to Chicago for a weekend bust. It was a real one. Hotel suite, champagne, dancing — and passion all over the place. I made the mistake of thinking it was love. He made the mistake of thinking he should be grateful. But on our wedding night, Tucker Fairbairn, I knew — that was only a month or so later — but I knew I had done Stowe Vashon just about the biggest hurt a woman can do to a man. And since — I have tried to be a good wife, to help him. He realizes that I had given him his first big break, and he has stayed grateful to me for it. But that's not *marriage,* Tuck. Of course, a man and woman, living in the same house, sharing the same bed — but it wasn't marriage, Tuck. It was hurt. To Stowe —"

"And to you, dear." He was sitting there, stunned at what she had been revealing to him. Had Carrie known these things? Partially, he supposed.

"I hurt everyone," Megan was saying bitterly. "Carrie too, because it was Carrie whom Stowe loved."

"She was just a kid . . ." Tuck reminded Megan. But, yes, Stowe Vashon had loved her. Tuck remembered that brief scene on Megan's wedding day.

"She was seventeen, and lovely," said Carrie's sister. "But there he was, married to me . . ."

"Don't put yourself down that way, Megan!" he cried angrily. "You're a great girl. You always have been."

"Yes. Great," she said bitterly. "I told myself that in those first months. I told myself that I had brains, and I could work things out. I would help Stowe — and I did try, Tuck. I bought clothes I knew he would like, things I'd hear him admire on other women. I kept a nice home for him. We had friends. And — I did everything I could think of or read about. I became an expert on how a woman could please her husband. I kept myself up. In appearance. I read the damnedest dull books so that I could talk to him, and to his friends. I worked to help him realize his hopes for life. He was made a member of the firm, we belonged to the right club. We went to symphony concerts and became friends of everything that needed friends — art museum, the University, even the zoo. But the main thing I wanted, and was sure that Stowe wanted, was a family, the child I desperately wanted to have — and had to wait five years to have. Every gynecologist in town knew me. I even considered insemination."

"You didn't!"

"I would have. But then Bob, dear little Bob, finally helped me. Helped us. Because it did help, Tuck. We both wanted him, we both welcomed him, we both loved him. But —"

Now, Tuck thought, they cannot face what their love for Bob had brought them.

Megan began to talk again. "It was frightening, from the first, how much Stowe loved that baby. Bob had brought love into our home. But not love for me. After five years of not having a child — I was happy in the baby. I loved him, I do love him. But he has made no difference in our marriage. That kind of love, Tuck, doesn't come through any valiant struggle. And our marriage continued to be a failure. A failure which I can take, but which Stowe cannot. He must win, he must succeed."

Abruptly, Tucker stood up. He went to the fire and lifted a log back into the flames. He now could read Stowe Vashon. Bob's illness, the cancer which was eating his son's strong limb, was failure. A thing which Stowe Vashon could not face, which he would not accept. And there it was. Spelled out in lines of black letters in this pleasant, sun-bright room.

Failure! A little boy, the victim of a man's conceit, of his self-pride.

"Megan," Tuck said roughly, "could I make myself a drink?"

She looked up, surprised. "Why, yes, of course, Tuck," she said. "I'll get whatever you want."

"I'll make it." He wanted to get off to himself, if only for the time it would take to break out ice cubes, to —

He had told Carrie that he would not fight Stowe Vashon with his fists. Well, it was a damn good thing the man was not at home at this minute. Because —

He thought about Stowe Vashon. He found the glass, he poured liquor from a Waterford decanter, he splashed ice cubes into it, and held the glass in his two hands. Strong hands, clever hands. Clean and lean fingers, the nails scrubbed to pale ovals.

Stowe Vashon! Tuck scarcely knew the man by sight. He remembered him at his wedding, smooth, red-blond hair, a well-fitting coat, and for that tiny interlude, with his arms about Carrie. Carrie, exquisite at seventeen. Carrie, the fine, strong woman who would be Tuck's wife, in all the ways that Megan knew about, had talked about, and never had had from Stowe Vashon. These last days — a week? Ten days? Tuck had seen the man briefly at the far end of a long hospital corridor. One figure among many. Once he thought he saw him get up abruptly and leave the coffee shop.

Speaking to this one and that, especially to Don Moore, once or twice to Carrie, and now to Megan, Dr. Fairbairn knew that the man, Stowe Vashon, was a successful lawyer. A member of one of the city's most prestigious firms. A man to do all things correctly. Carrie had told him that. But Tuck still did not know him. He stood looking down into the amber liquid in the glass he held cupped in his hands.

At a Staff meeting about Bob's case, Tuck had heard one of the doctors speak half-admiringly of Stowe Vashon. He couldn't understand why he should be so opposed to surgery. Oh, yes, for a child to lose a leg was a terrific thing! But "Vashon is a brain. You know," he'd said, leaning across the table, "he's the sort of lawyer one calls *Esquire!*"

There had been some laughter at that, Tuck recalled, but — He went to the window, and now he tasted the drink which he had mixed. He really did not care much for whiskey, but something had to be done about his whirling thoughts.

He was remembering the wedding again, the people, the laughter and the talk — some things that had been said; he could not select the right words. But they were there, back in his memory, back in his thoughts. Was it possible that Carrie Reynolds had loved the man whom her sister had married?

Could Carrie possibly love a man who could not handle failure? Who would not face failure?

Failure, disappointment, was a part of life. Everyone met it, and though perhaps hurt and humiliated by it, everyone must learn to live with it. One learned from failure, and built his life upon what he had learned. A man had to learn those lessons, and if he did not . . .

Illness, sometimes, *was* failure. But only when it developed through neglect, or reckless carelessness. If Stowe Vashon now would not care for his small son, there indeed would be a failure. Carrie would know those truths.

Only minutes ago, Tuck had agreed with Megan that he and Carrie did know —

"read" each other, their thoughts and their beliefs. So, now he knew that Carrie did not love a man like Stowe Vashon. He could put that doubt to rest. For all time.

He looked down at his glass, surprised to find it in his hands. With three long steps, he took it to the divider between the living room and the family room. He set it down on the counter, turned, and came back. He knelt on the thick carpet beside Megan and took her hand in his. It trembled a little.

"I don't like, Megan," he said gently, "the things I feel must be said and done to you and Stowe. But —

"Who was the guy in the Bible who said, 'It's like a fire inside me, a burning in my bones'?"

She was gazing at him. "Jeremiah?" she asked softly.

Tuck nodded. "It could have been Jeremiah. Any way, I have that burning in my bones. I don't like saying these hard things which I have to say. But there they are.

"Bob, the dear little boy, has cancer. A bad kind of cancer. It can and will spread rapidly through his body. Amputation is a fearful thing to contemplate on such a child. But death is even more fearful. So an A/K is the only thing we can do, Megan. It is all we can do with any hope of saving that young life. Following with chemotherapy, and other measures, the outlook is hopeful if we now work swiftly. And there it is, Megan, the hard thing which I have to say to you."

For a brief second, she put her forehead down against his shoulder. "Thank you, Jeremiah . . ." she whispered. "Thank you."

"Now!" he said, standing up. "We have things to do. And the very first thing is to figure a way to give Bob the care we know he has to have."

She started to stand too, then sat down quickly, her face suddenly ashen. He caught her arm. "Megan?" he asked anxiously.

She shook her head. "I was dizzy for a minute," she said. "I have been so worried lately . . ."

"Of course you have. Here, sit with me on the couch. And together maybe we can think of what we could say or do to get this matter straightened out. For myself, I'd say or do almost anything. Pick up Bob, take him to o.r. — crazy things like that. Have Stowe declared incompetent — But we both know there are limits. I have tried to think — Should I tell you, Megan, to get a divorce from Vashon, and be given custody of your child? Though that would take too long."

"Besides," she said softly, "the only advice you can give me, ethically, is medical advice."

That was true. Had Stowe reminded her of that? Possibly he had.

"Would you," he asked, then stopped, and sat thinking for a minute. "Would you consider going to court and asking — no, *getting* — a court order for this life-saving surgery?"

She turned to look at him, her face brightening.

"Could I do that?" she asked eagerly. "You would help me?"

"With the professional testimony? Yes, I sure would."

"Then maybe I could do it. How would I go about it, Tuck? Do you know?"

"Oh, yes. The necessity comes up every now and then. You'd need to make application, you'd need to establish that Stowe has refused . . ."

Still gazing at him, the bright hope faded from her eyes and from her face. "I would need a lawyer," she said slowly. "Wouldn't I?"

"Yes, of course."

"Then . . ." And tears came into her eyes. "What lawyer would I get? I can't embarrass Stowe in his own profession, Tuck."

He stared at her in disbelief. "Megan Reynolds!" he shouted. "You can't mean what you are saying!"

"You don't know Stowe. His profession means everything to him. There probably are lawyers who would help me in a suit against my husband. But — well, I just could not do it."

"Not even for Bob?"

Now she wept stormily. She would, she sobbed, do anything for Bob. She thought she would. But when it came actually to ask — to face Stowe in a court of law — in his own field — she knew herself. She knew that she could not go through with a thing like that!

"No one would blame you —"

"They would blame Stowe. And what would that do to him, Tuck? What position would he have — Oh, no! I could not do that, Tuck. I know I couldn't. We will have to find another way. You say you want to pick Bob up and take him to the operating room. Could I possibly take him out of the hospital and get on a plane and —"

"You're talking hysterically, Megan," he said, wanting to quiet her. He could not persuade an emotional woman —

She nodded, sobbed, and mopped the tears from her face.

"All right," he said, when she had quieted. "Let's take another look at this situation. Here you and Stowe are, parents of a mortally sick little boy. You want to help him, Stowe cannot face the idea of amputation. You don't love each other; you told me that you did not. So why doesn't Bob come first? Why don't you consider him above this man you say —"

"Tuck," she said firmly, "I don't remember just what I said. I told you I had hurt Stowe by letting him marry me when he didn't love me. I may have said we don't love each other. But that doesn't mean —"

He turned to look at her. And his face was angry. "Are you trying to tell me that *you* love him? That you —"

She was nodding her head up and down. "Women are crazy people, Tucker," she said solemnly. "I know that, and you do."

"And you love Stowe Vashon."

"Yes. I always have. I worked — I hoped I could make him love me. I thought when we married . . . But just the same, I loved him, and I always have."

Tuck stood up. He paced the room. He stared out of the window, he stood before the fire on the hearth, and stared down at it. "Never in a thousand years," he muttered. Finally he turned to look at Megan, who still sat, white-faced and pitiful on the couch.

"I am thinking," he said sternly, "of a little redheaded boy who needs you, who needs me. He clutches a bright blue bathrobe close in his arms because he is afraid. He knows something is wrong, he needs some grownups to help him. And you —" He stepped toward her. "Don't you love *Bob*, Megan?" he shouted. "*Don't* you?"

Later, telling Carrie of the awful things he had done and said to Megan, he told that "she just dissolved, Carrie. She really did. It frightened me, to see her melt down into the corner of that couch."

"And you gathered her up and comforted her. I know how you would do. Oh, Tuck, I could have told you. She does love Bob, but her feeling for Stowe — I could kill the man, but —"

His lips silenced the words on her lips. "*Shhhh,*" he said. "We will find an answer to Megan's question."

She searched his face. "What question did she find to ask you?"

Tuck shook his head. "One that was damn hard to answer, Carrie, my darling. She asked me how a mother can know what she should do."

"And you comforted her. You held her

warm against your big, strong body, and comforted her. I wonder if Stowe has ever —"

Tuck tried to smile. "Megan told me that you were a lucky girl, Carrie."

"Oh, she did, did she?" cried Carrie. "Well, don't get conceited about it! And there's another thing. Maybe I just might find out how jealous I can get of these women you comfort."

"Aw, Carrie!"

She kissed him. "Did you find any sort of hope to give Megan?" she asked.

"Yes. I told her that I was going to find a way to help Bob."

"But, Tuck . . ."

"I told her what I'm sure as hell going to have to tell you. But now I'll tell you that I have a staff meeting at four and I am just about to be late."

He was late for the meeting. "Someone always stops me," he explained when he came in and sat down at the table, the only person there not in hospital whites. "There's no rule about it," he answered a comment.

"Did you run all the way, Tuck?" another doctor asked.

"Since noon. Since noon," said Tucker,

opening the folder which his secretary had provided for him. He leaned forward to address the Chief of Medical Services. "I have a matter to add to your agenda, sir," he said.

"Now, Fairbairn . . ."

"Crises have a way of coming up around here without much regard for agenda," said Dr. Fairbairn firmly.

"Yes, I know they do. Is yours one to put at the head of my list?"

"Not unless this session goes on all night."

"The dear Lord forbid," said Dr. West earnestly.

These meetings could deal with any or all of the problems which could arise in a complex the size of theirs. An epidemic in Children's, the rising cost of food in Diet and Nutrition . . . Each service must make statistical reports. And today there was a cleansing bit of levity when Outpatient made his report on what, at the last meeting, had seemed to indicate an epidemic among its women regulars. "Bullous erythema," he identified the problem. Blisters on the women's legs.

"Only women?" asked someone, and Tuck stirred impatiently in his chair. Why must some character always hold things up with silly questions?

Though Outpatient was handling the matter. "That was in my last report," he said mildly. "I was getting quite a few patients suffering from these red blisters. Some came in voluntarily, some were referred. It puzzled me. And then I was intrigued by the fact that the women seemed to know each other. Not friends precisely, but they would greet each other. I made careful notes and cross references." He was smiling broadly. "I found that most of them were cleaning women and that they all rode a certain bus that served the area where they worked. It's one of those manmade projects. Called Earth Town, built on a landfill out into the lake, I think. They want industries, they build office towers to serve the area. And these women clean there. They work from five in the morning until eight. There's this special bus for their accommodation; they transfer to it from the city buses."

The doctors were all getting impatient. Watches were being looked at. Some had rounds to make, some were ready to go home . . .

Tucker Fairbairn began to turn a pencil end for end, and to whistle soundlessly through his pursed lips.

Outpatient nodded to him. "I'll just say,

and not as dramatically, I fear, as some of you gentlemen could do it that I did discover the cause of our bullous erythema."

"Let's have it then," said Tuck. "In twenty-five words or less."

"Oh, much less, doctor. The cause was quite simple. The darned bus, an old one but serviceable for its purpose, was found to be infested with bedbugs." He sat back, smiling.

Everyone in the room straightened to attention. There was laughter, there was argument — it couldn't be! — it damn well could be! Did one ever get bitten by a bedbug? All right, then. You sit on a seat of some woven plastic stuff, and the warmth — something — bullous erythema. Yes, sir!

"All right," said Dr. West. "There's your joke for the day, Fairbairn. What else do you have on your mind?"

"Not bedbugs," said Tuck, taking a sheet of paper from his folder. "I have a serious case of a child." And he tersely told in technical terms about Bob Vashon. The disease, the test results, the diagnosis, the prognosis. He concluded by saying that immediate surgery was imperative. "Today I detected a slight tremor in his limb and in one hand. That could indicate a blood clot. We *cannot* wait on this surgery if we are to save the child from a spread of the cancer, and his death."

"And your problem, Dr. Fairbairn?" asked Dr. Humphrey, though he and a large proportion of the people around the table knew what that problem was. No one was laughing about bedbugs now.

Tuck stood up. He told about the parents, he told about the father's refusal even to discuss the case with the doctor of record. His refusal to agree to surgery. He told of his arguments with the mother, and identified her. It was a sad case. And he had reached what must be the limit of any doctor's ability to help a patient in desperate circumstances. "I must tell you that I myself am about to go to court and ask that the child be made a ward of the court, and surgery ordered."

The room became very still. "That can be a bombshell, Fairbairn," said Dr. West.

"Yes, sir. I am not asking for any action to be taken here. I am only telling you what I plan to do, at my discretion as a surgeon. It can be a bombshell, as you say, or a great service. I hope the last will be the result in any case. I would protect the Complex in all ways. This surgery would be done strictly on my own initiative."

"Vashon could sue you, ruin you."

"Yes, he could. In fact, I think he might. He is a smart lawyer, and I think he can hurt me. But to nothing like the extent that he is hurting his son."

No one now was looking at his watch. All eyes were on the tall man who stood so tensely, yet quietly, too, and declared his intent. Tall, his dark head held high, his dark eyes shining with resolve, his mouth and jaw firm. White turtle-neck sweater, houndstooth sports coat, brown slacks, the surgeons saw a man in o.r. green doing the skilled surgery which had saved so many lives, which held out hope for those who would have need of his care in the future, which had taught so many younger men.

Some of the Staff knew him better than did others, but they all liked Tucker Fairbairn, and admired him. Trusted him. And each was asking, "Would I do what Tuck is proposing? He's tops in his field, but — would I do it? Would I risk so much?"

As many answered *yes* as said *no*. All said that to do such a thing took guts.

Here and there Carrie was mentioned, and Tuck's relationship to the family involved. But that would not cause Tuck to do this. He would make the same decision for any child brought to him; he was that sort of doctor. "Besides, in my case," said one man, "planning to marry the kid's aunt would hold my hand." Yes, that could be true.

Dr. West, Chief of Medical Services, sat gazing at Tuck, allowing the talk to buzz around the table for as much as five minutes. The Chief was not a young man, his hair had silvered and thinned through years of medical services. But this evening he was feeling an excitement which he had thought lost to him. Doctors these days, doctors in these huge, efficient steel and glass and stone complexes, he feared, were losing the need to fight to save an individual patient.

He scratched his ear, and straightened in his chair. "When do you plan to do all this, Tuck?" he asked.

"I have an appointment with a certain judge for eight o'clock this evening, sir."

"Very well," said Dr. West. He turned to the secretary. "You won't need anything recorded beyond the agenda," he said firmly. "And that ended with Outpatient's bedbugs."

This time few laughed. Tuck had taken the break to escape the room. He didn't want the matter hashed over, though he was planning to see Carrie, to tell her.

And of course, early the next morning, he did see her, he did tell her. Of his interview with the Judge, of the message he had had, and especially what he was now planning.

"The Judge read all my papers, he talked to several people, lawyers, doctors, I don't know who-all —"

"Megan and Stowe," said Carrie softly. She was in o.r. green, the terrible dishcover cap on her head, showing better than any hairdo or makeup could the pure beauty of her face. Tuck had asked her to come to his office.

Gazing at her, Tuck slowly nodded. "Yes," he said. "I suppose he talked to them twice. Once, to get their side of the situation, once to tell them that he had decided — the *Court* had decided to give the mother the right to make the decision in this case."

Carrie had already heard the news, but his telling her still made the color drain from her face, and her eyes widen. "You are a very brave man, Tucker Fairbairn," she said softly. "May I kiss you?"

"Any time," he said gruffly. "But don't do it because I'm brave. I've done so much shaking in my boots these last twenty-four hours. In fact, I am still shaking. I have hated every word, every step that had to be said and taken. I kept wishing something would break —"

"It did. You decided to take the only step

which would save Bob's life. Which could save it. Even Stowe will come around to thanking you."

"I hope you're right. I never thought I would welcome the chance to cut off a little boy's leg — but that's the good part of all this, of course."

"Is there a bad part?"

"There sure is. Just now, the publicity. The talk, talk, talk here in the hospital. The arguments . . . The advice . . ."

Carrie nodded. "Yes," she said. "That's how I first heard of the court order. Every intern and nurse's aide knows what you should have done."

"Don't get into it, Carrie."

"Oh, I shan't. Not even with — But, Tuck, darling, can you *imagine* what is being said out in Edgewood between Stowe and Megan?"

Megan knew. She definitely knew what was being said and done between her and Stowe. When she came back from her bedtime visit with Bob, Stowe had met her at the door. She was, he said icily, to call a certain number. He would not even try to stop her. She looked at him curiously. "The great stone face." She knew he was called that. During certain trials he had been so

160

described in the newspaper. Tonight . . .

She took the slip of paper which he handed to her. She slipped out of her coat and went to the kitchen to use that telephone. Stowe followed her, not speaking again, but watching her. Watching her, his gray-green eyes like stone.

Her voice trembled when she discovered that she was speaking to a certain Judge, that she was being asked asked . . .

Tuck. Tuck was going to find a way to help Bob! That was all that mattered. She turned her back on Stowe, and answered the questions.

She would never forget the appearance of her kitchen desk wedged in between the sink and the door of the utility room, the yellow pencil, the pad of paper which reminded her to buy bacon and coffee. And Stowe behind her, just standing there, listening, protesting without speaking one word, or making one sound.

But Bob was such a sick little boy! That evening he had not talked very much. He wanted to be cuddled, and asked if he could go home, and then drowsed against her shoulder.

It hurt to see him so. This whole thing did hurt so dreadfully. From the first, when she had guessed that something was wrong with Bob — if Stowe had shared her hurt, it would have been more bearable — but his hurt had taken the form of rebellion. He would not believe — he did not want anything *done* . . .

If Stowe had tried to comfort her, and reassure the child . . . He went to see Bob in the hospital. Alone, he went. What did he find to say to the boy? Megan could find very little. She knew that his leg hurt; no, she didn't like shots either. Tuck was a doctor. So was Dr. Moore. They would take care of Bob's leg —

Now, after quite a bit of talk, she must set the telephone down and turn to face Stowe's cold eyes. Then he talked. He knew what that damned doctor was up to. As if Stowe Vashon needed the Children's Court to tell him what to do for his son! Had Megan told Fairbairn . . . ?

What part had Carrie played?

She need not answer. Stowe did not wait for answers.

It was a dreadful scene, a dreadful night. Tuck must have known it would be. The Judge had said that he knew Mrs. Vashon had refused to go over her husband's head in making the decision. He would have preferred, and the doctors would much prefer, that the parents be in accord on this. He hoped they might yet agree to accept the medical verdict. Without the surgery, the boy would surely die. So this effort must be made to save a child's life.

It was a dreadful scene, a dreadful night in that pretty, comfortable house. Stowe said all the horrid things; Megan must hear them and hold fast to her resolve to help Bob.

Yes, she agreed, he would be crippled, but he would be *alive!*

And yes, he might die even with the surgery. All surgery held risks. But this surgery was more chance than risk. This was his only chance! And he was to have it. She would no more deny it to her child than she would deny food to him.

Then — Stowe refused to speak another word. And that hurt too. All night he sat and stared before him, and would not speak. Megan went to bed. And lay there, staring, feeling the hurt which had to be there, but which could have been borne if Stowe would have been one bit softer, if he —

So, the whole thing did hurt so dreadfully! Megan supposed it was hurting Stowe as much as it hurt her. The very illness of their child hurt, and this quarrel, this terrible row! There was no place to turn from it, no help for it.

If Stowe loved her, and would try to comfort her . . . But he did not love her, and never had. And finally, toward the end of that dreadful night, she told the iron-faced man that she knew he had never loved her.

Then Stowe spoke. "I have stayed with you," he said tightly.

There had been a time when he almost did not "stay." Megan had known about that time. It was before Bob was conceived and born.

But this night, she agreed that he had indeed "stayed." Now, she said, she wished that he had not. That he would not.

He stared at her. "Shouldn't you be the one to leave?" he asked.

Then it was Megan who was ice-cold. Her face, her voice. "No," she said thinly. "I couldn't leave. I can't."

"Almost any court would give you the child."

"I bore your child because I loved you, Stowe. I cannot, I never could, leave you because I do love you. Why, God only knows. And to admit it is the most humbling thing a woman ever can do."

He got up from the chair then, went to the window and opened the curtains. A very thin line of light was beginning to show beyond the treetops and behind the houses.

"Today," he said, as if announcing the coming of that day, "today you are going to that hospital and sign their damned papers. You say you love me. You say you love our child. And yet you would go through with this awful thing."

She sighed. "I have to do it, Stowe," she said wearily. "I can't stop from doing it now."

"You could," he said, turning to pass her. "You can. And if you cannot, Megan . . ." He turned, and she thought, at last, he would touch her, perhaps hurt her, even . . . "If you can't, Megan," he repeated, "I promise you that I will break the doctor who touches a knife to my son, the doctor who is giving you this chance to mutilate him."

Megan faced him. "You cannot mean Tuck!" she whispered.

"Of course I mean *Tuck!*" He spat the name venomously at her.

"But why?" she asked. "I don't understand you at all, Stowe Vashon. Why should you react as you are doing? Grief, yes. I understand that. I myself grieve, terribly, that this thing has come to us. But hatred of the doctor who would and can help Bob — I do not understand you at all."

He turned away, and walked to the kitchen. He took the telephone book from the shelf and looked up a number. Megan watched him. He had not undressed that night, his shirt collar was wrinkled, and the sweater vest he wore hung loosely. His face was gray and lined with fatigue.

He dialed a number, and waited. She could hear the ring signal, and then a voice.

"Dr. Tucker Fairbairn?" said Stowe.

Megan gasped.

"This is Stowe Vashon," said her husband, "the father of the child you are planning to mutilate. No! I will not listen! But I mean to tell you, and I shall tell you that if you operate on my son, you will be sorry . . ."

Tuck's voice broke in. "I know you are threatening me, Vashon," he said firmly, loudly. "You are making a personal thing of this. Whereas my only consideration is the child's life."

"And you think mine should be?" said Stowe, his voice acid with his bitterness.

"I believe so." Megan heard Tuck's voice say that. She turned and almost ran up to the bedroom, to dress, to go to the hospital. She must protect her child.

And so Tuck called Carrie and asked her to make a chance to come to his office before surgery that morning. He told her of his action, and they speculated on the sort of night Megan had spent with Stowe.

"When . . . ?"

"I've scheduled it for Monday."

"Shall I ask Megan to stay with me? Do you think Stowe is dangerous?"

"She can stay right here at the hospital."

Yes, she could. There were accommodations for mothers to stay with a child should that seem helpful.

"Did you see the Judge, Tuck?" she asked. "What I really mean is, did he see you?"

"Yes."

"That's good."

"Why?" He smiled, faintly curious.

"If you had a mirror I could show you. You are strong, and show it. You are sincere, people believe what you say."

"Not Stowe Vashon."

"Oh, Tuck. The man — he must be insane."

"He could be. Paranoid, at least. Talking to Megan about him — remember, I don't know him. But talking about him, she made me believe that he considered the crippling of a child — his child — a personal failure. And Megan says Stowe cannot endure failure of any size or importance."

167

Carrie drew a deep breath of relief. "Then that must be why he is taking the stand he does."

"I think it must be. He feels, perhaps, that he is being kind to the child, that it would be kindness to any child, not to let him live as a cripple."

"But that is insane!"

"No. It is really a form of euthanasia. The o.b. men get this reaction, this situation, from fathers, and sometimes mothers — very frequently from grandmothers — when they deliver a defective child."

"Oh, dear."

He put his arm around her. "We had to talk about it, sweetheart."

"Yes, of course we did. And I know what all this is costing you."

"The Judge brought up the personal angle. I think I persuaded him that I would and do feel the same way about any child in Bob's situation."

"I hope you did convince him. Megan thinks Stowe doesn't love Bob. Not enough, anyway."

"I know. She told me that yesterday. That she had decided their child meant nothing to him, that he would be ashamed of him crippled, and actually hate him."

"Do you believe that?"

"I think Megan believes it. Personally, I don't know, Carrie. I don't know Stowe Vashon. He's been avoiding any confrontation with me.

"He avoids all the doctors. The nurses — even little Bob — have noticed that. He comes to see Bob, but if a doctor comes into the ward, Stowe leaves."

Six

The surgery was scheduled for nine on Monday morning. This was Thursday. The notice went on Bob's chart, on the desk boards, up in letters on the big board over the desk in the surgical suite. Memos were given to the individual members of the team, or crew.

Carrie was not so notified, and she asked about her omission. "Go off in a corner and think about it," the Surgical Superintendent told her.

"I have spent so much time in corners on that case . . ."

"I know you have, dearie."

"I suppose I could observe?"

"That's up to Dr. F."

"He'll tell me to stay with Megan."

"Yes. Reckon he will. Reckon you had better do it too."

Carrie's eyes filled with tears. "We are all so worried!" she blurted.

"We used to have an orderly around here,

Carrie," said the Supe. "A colored man, getting old, but still a hard worker. And I used to hear him tell families, folks like you — 'Ailin' ain't always dyin',' he'd say. And most of the time he was right!"

So Carrie would stay with Megan.

At a Surgical Staff meeting where the necessity for a court order was briefly discussed, it was forbidden the personnel to speak of the matter. They were not to talk of it among themselves. Such orders were fairly common, but often they served to increase tension; throughout the hospital particular notice was given to the ward where Bob Vashon was a patient, heads turned when Megan went in and out, the nurses at the floor desk took an especial interest in the child's chart. Carrie was watched, and of course Dr. Fairbairn.

Megan decided against staying at the hospital on Thursday night; Stowe came home as usual and sat down to dinner with the announcement that he did not want to talk. He had dressed in his usual meticulous fashion, but he still looked gray and tired. Megan guessed that she did too. That night she slept in the guest room.

Out at his cabin, Tuck split logs of wood and carried them inside for a fire. He wished he had brought Carrie home with him. He hated so much pressure because of one case. It was not an ideal way to practice surgery. He was fond of Bob, but when he made rounds he joked with the child, or mildly scolded him, exactly as he did the other children. The surgery would go the same way. Yet even Bob seemed to know that his case was somewhat different from that of his companions on Ortho-surgical. He asked the nurse to tell him what she wrote on his chart.

"Want me to read the whole thing to you?" she asked pertly.

"Does it have pictures?"

"No pictures."

"Well, you can start. But I like books with pictures."

The young woman nodded. "They are better," she agreed. "Well, it says here that this chart, or book if we are going to call it that, is named Robert Vashon."

"Bob," the child corrected her.

"The chart says Robert."

"Go on."

"O.K. It says this Robert Vashon is a well-nourished white male . . ."

"Boy?"

"Boy. And this column shows what the thermometer says whenever we read it."

"That's dull."

"So it is. Why don't you put on your earphones and listen to the music? I'll rub your back."

Tuck had overheard the interchange. The nurse was making a valiant try at being casual. They all were. But of course, in spite of the specific orders, talk did flourish. Everyone did some talking, and everyone asked everyone else how Dr. Fairbairn had been able to go to the court.

Tonight he sat lonely before the fire, and wondered about that himself. "How could he do it?" they asked, the nurse, the kitchen maid, Dr. Billings . . .

A fair question. It was "fair" when Tuck asked it. How could he do it?

He stirred, and opened the book on his knee. That was a fair question. Asked by himself. *How could he do it?* The Judge had asked it; Tuck had put it to himself in a dozen ways. And the answer had been, the answer still was, "What else was there to do?"

But he had another question, which he had overheard from o.r. that morning while he was studying the x-rays of a hip joint which he was about to replace. "How does Carrie feel about Tuck's going to court?"

Well, how did she feel? She said she thought him courageous. She seemed to agree with what he had done. She even attempted to judge his own feelings. But as had the girls scurrying about in o.r. he faced up to the next question.

"What if . . . ?"

What if what? Oh, a dozen things. All of them unpleasant to contemplate. And he would not contemplate them. He opened the book, which was a novel with about a hundred characters whom he was finding it difficult to identify.

"Any scrub nurse," he had heard an older voice say firmly, "knows that any prime surgeon has had all the emotionalism trained out of him."

Then what was left? A rock. Yes, a rock. The o.r. girls accepted that, and Dr. Fairbairn had better accept it too.

He threw the thick book at the couch, stood up, and decided that he would take a walk. But no, he guessed not. It was raining. A cold, shivery winter rain.

So he would make himself a fried egg sandwich, and have another go at the damn book. But he did wish he knew if Carrie could really love a rock.

He could ask her the next morning; she was scheduled for his o.r.

But the next morning, Carrie's question

put all else out of his head. She was personally attending the establishment of their patient, a large and nervous woman, on the table. Sometimes a word from the surgeon quieted this kind. It did that morning. "She thought someone else might operate," Carrie whispered as they went away from the table.

"A popular fiction around these places," said the doctor.

"Have you a minute, Tuck?"

"I don't know. My clock's in my sock."

Her eyes went to the large, round clock on the wall. He laughed. "What is it?"

"Did you see Bob this morning?"

"No." It was early.

"He wants to go home. He told me to ask you. He seems to think if I kiss you . . ."

"Smart boy. But, gee, pops, Carrie!"

"I know. I reminded him that he was to have his operation on Monday. But it seems his bed at home bounces better than the crib . . . Could he? Just for, say, thirty-six hours?"

"Oh, Carrie . . ."

She was wearing a white apron-sort of garment; her green scrub smock would tie over it. But for now, her soft arms were bare to the shoulder. He touched one swiftly as they walked out into the hall to talk.

Her upward smile was wistful. "There are so many problems," she agreed. "Bob knows he can't stay at home. He says he will watch out the car window so he will know how to come back to the hospital."

Tuck smiled. "Good for him! But, of course, Carrie, there are — as you say — a great many problems. Things he cannot do."

"Like that bed bouncing. Yes, I know. Couldn't I go with him as nurse? Maybe not in uniform . . ."

"I think there should be a nurse, Carrie. But —"

"I've thought of Stowe."

"And what he might do. His threats."

"He is a great respecter of the law, Tuck. He won't kidnap Bob, if that is your mind."

"He can be extremely nasty to Bob's nurse."

"Yes, he could be. Maybe I should wear a uniform. Though Megan thinks Stowe might not even stay in the house while Bob's there."

Tuck frowned. "How *can* he act the way he does, Carrie?"

"I've done a lot of thinking about that. Megan has too. She thinks a man's love can be so hard, so hurtful that it takes over his entire personality. She thinks that is the way he loves Bob. He may stay at home, or he may find an excuse not to be there. But in any case, he won't hurt the child, and he won't hurt me. Incidentally, whether Stowe told him or not, Bob knows it is his mother who thinks he should have the operation."

"Does he know about the leg?" They were walking slowly down the corridor, passing the carts, the hurrying nurses, the man wiping up some mess which had been spilled. Now they turned to go back.

"Does Bob know about his leg?" Tuck asked again.

"No, I don't think so."

"Stowe should tell him."

Carrie stopped and turned to look directly at Tuck. "He won't!" she whispered fiercely. "He wouldn't!"

"Then I'll have to do it."

"You don't think Megan? Or me?" Her face was white.

He shook his head. "This is man's work," he said.

"But I can . . ."

"Oh, yes, you can go home with him. I'll tell the Surgery nurse's secretary . . . What's her name?"

"Mary," said Carrie gently. "One of those unusual names."

Tuck squeezed her soft arm, and turned into Scrub.

Bob did go home, and the family accommodated itself as best it could to what his visit meant. Megan baked cookies for him. Stowe played a game with him. But there wasn't much bed bouncing. The child limped badly, and was tired. On Sunday morning he was ready to help pack his small bag. A pair of pajamas with trains printed on it, his precious blue robe. "I'll just wear my slippers," he said. "They feel good on my feet." He was thinner, his eyes bigger.

"Have you had a good time?" Megan asked him.

"Gee, pops, yes! Milk out of my own cup, and peanut butter. But I said I'd come back. As soon as Carrie fixes lunch for me and her."

"We'll all go with you."

"That's good. I'll play with the other kids, and Joe's dog, when I come home again after the op'ration."

"Sure you will."

"Tuck says I'll feel better."

"Tuck should know."

Stowe turned abruptly away, going into the bedroom. Megan followed him. Carrie was calling to Bob that his lunch was ready.

"He has enjoyed being at home," Megan told her husband, who was standing at the window. "I think he needed to be reassured that these familiar things were still here."

"Are you going to tell him what will happen to him when he gets back to the damned hospital?" Stowe asked tightly.

"Should I?" asked Megan. She stood at the foot of the bed, not going close to him.

He turned enough to look at her face. "Could you?" he asked, horrified.

"Together we could, I think. Maybe."

"What could we tell him? He's only four years old."

"We could tell him we are giving him a chance for life." Megan's voice rang clearly.

"Are you?" Stowe asked bitterly. "*Are* you?"

"I believe we are."

An hour later they were on their way, Bob sitting beside his father, his big eyes watchful, but he wasn't talking very much. "That's our hospital," he pointed out when they reached the Complex. "The low one. It was built for little boys with sore legs."

Stowe opened his lips as if to speak. But he did not.

"He'll park the car," Bob told his mother when she came to help the child out, and take the small bag. "Dad doesn't like hospitals very much."

"They make people get well," said Megan, reaching for the boy's hand.

"I know how to get upstairs from here," said Bob.

"Well, wait a minute, and you can show me." Megan went to the desk; she must sign the patient in. She hesitated over her signature, but wrote it steadily. *Megan R. Vashon. (Mrs. Stowe)* That was her signature. If Stowe wouldn't . . .

When she turned from the desk, she found Bob talking to Dr. Stirling, the pediatrician, whom Bob knew very well. He reminded his mother that he did.

She smiled at the doctor. "How are you?" she asked.

"Oh," he said, "pediatricians are never very well. The children bring their colds to us, and leave the things behind. I take mine home to my family — and you really should hear a convention of pediatricians. Such coughing and goings-on you won't hear any place else!"

Megan smiled rewardingly and turned to see where Bob had got to. Dr. Stirling went with her to see if he could help with the child who was watching some goldfish in a small fountain's pool. With him was another boy, about eight.

Bob pointed to him eagerly. "This is Leslie," he said. "*He* had a sore leg and now he walks on scrutches, but he won't after Christmas. That's keen, isn't it?"

"It certainly is," said Megan. "We'd better go up stairs now, Bob."

"Can I help you?" Dr. Stirling asked the boy.

"No, sir. I limp pretty bad, but I can walk. Dr. Tuck's going to take care of that, you know. And he sure will!"

Dr. Stirling smiled and nodded. "He sure will," he repeated firmly.

Upstairs Bob was disappointed that he would not return to the ward with other children but, until his surgery, would occupy a small private room and have his own nurse.

He viewed this young woman dubiously. "My Aunt Carrie's a nurse," he said.

"Oh, yes, I know she is. But she works in the operating room. I just take care of boys like you."

"Well . . ." said Bob, still unconvinced. "But I can undress and put on my own pajamas."

"That will be a big help," said the nurse.

But just then Carrie arrived with a couple of hand puppets for Bob. Tigger and Eeyore, and the child was entranced. "Oh, gee, pops," he said. "Can I make them talk?"

"As soon as you are in bed," Carrie told him firmly.

So Bob let his mother help him undress, and he was happily making his new friends talk when Tuck came into the room.

"How're you, Bob?" he asked, looking at the chart.

"I'm fine. D'you see Tigger? He says he doesn't like the hospital, but Eeyore does. Eeyore likes to stay in bed."

"Lazy fellow, isn't he?" said Tuck, bending over the child, swiftly feeling his limbs, listening to his heart and lungs. "Did you have a good time at home?"

"Pretty good. I didn't feel like running much, or riding my three-wheeler."

"I know. But maybe next time you will feel that way."

"You bet," said Bob, busy with the puppets which he told to say good-bye to Tuck.

Waving back, Tuck went on down the corridor, turning into ward and room as he progressed.

Megan was sitting beside Bob's bed, reading to him, when Stowe came into the room. She touched her finger to her lips. "We hope he'll get a nap," she said softly.

But Bob must show the puppets to his

father, and was still doing this when Dr. Moore came in.

He was a tall, dark-haired man who wore black-rimmed glasses. Bob called him "Doc," as did most of the children in the area.

Immediately Stowe got to his feet and prepared to leave. But today he said, surprising Megan, that he wanted to speak to the doctor.

"You can go out in the hall," Bob instructed him. "That's mostly where Dads and Moms talk to the doctors. Anyway, I have to take a nap."

Dr. Moore raised an eyebrow to Megan, but closely followed Stowe into the corridor. He wished Tuck could be around. But immediately it became evident that Bob's father thought he was Dr. Fairbairn. The personnel were supposed to wear name plates, but Don Moore had none on the white jacket he had pulled on over his pale yellow shirt and dark green tie. On Sunday things were a little relaxed.

And he thought it more important to listen to what Vashon had to say. Later he could explain the mistaken identity; it often happened, and often it made little difference if the doctor were the Chief or his trusted assistant.

If it did make a difference there would be time enough . . .

Stowe walked a dozen paces away from the door to Bob's room. Then he turned to face the doctor, to lean toward him a little. "Are you really going through with this thing?" he demanded in a fierce whisper.

"Do you mean the leg surgery?" asked Dr. Moore. "Yes, we plan to do it."

"When?" Stowe's green eyes probed the doctor's face.

"In a day or two." It was scheduled for nine the next morning but that could be changed.

"I am the boy's father, and you know how I feel."

"Yes, I do, Mr. Vashon," said Dr. Moore. "But you should listen to the experts in this field."

"Meaning you!"

"A half-dozen experts have examined and observed Bob."

"And I should let them tell me . . ."

"Now, look. Why don't you put this situation into your own field, Vashon? You're a lawyer. I happen to know that you consult lawbooks, you seek precedents, you discuss the case on trial with judges and other lawyers, seeking the best advice —"

"I am not about to cut off a child's leg!"

"But you were trying to send a man to prison! Or to free him from charges."

"It's not at all the same thing."

"It is when we consider the value of expert professional advice."

"Well, I can tell you — I can *promise* you — that you will be sorry when you have done this awful thing to my boy."

"Maybe," said Dr. Moore quietly. "I *know* we shall be sorry if we don't do it."

"But you'll be the one holding the knife."

"I'll be one of a team," said Donald Moore, still quietly, his mind flashing a swift picture of the green-gowned, white-masked specialists who would surround the patient on the table. Scrub nurse, circulating, anaesthetist, surgeon, his assistant, the resident probably . . . The doctor began to speak, and list these people. "Everyone specifically trained to do the work," he said. "Experienced. We'll have a pediatric specialist to assist us. A pediatric surgeon."

"Why?"

"Because Bob is a small child. A child's blood vessels are small, and sometimes a specially trained man is helpful. We probably shan't need him, but he'll be there as a precaution. Just as we always have a cardiac team ready whenever surgery is performed. The way a fireman surveys and watches a theater when you attend a show."

"This is not a show!" cried Stowe in anguish.

"Mr. Vashon . . ." One had to pity the man.

Stowe started to walk down the hall. "And if you go through with it," he shouted over his shoulder, "I'll see to it that you regret it!"

Dr. Moore hurried to keep up with him. "Is that a threat, sir?" he asked.

Stowe turned on him a look of pure hatred. "Yes, sir," he said. "It is." He stepped into the elevator, and the door closed.

"It all happened so fast," said the floor nurse at the desk. The white-faced women there with her nodded in agreement. "They came down the hall, talking — and all of a sudden this man —"

"Mr. Vashon," said another nurse.

"Yes, Mr. Vashon. He began to shout at poor Dr. Moore —"

"Threatening him," said another young woman.

"I think he should be held," said the Floor Head.

They said this to Dr. Moore when he came around to sign out before going home.

"I've been shouted at before," said Don

quietly. "Anyway, he thought I was Fairbairn."

Tuck was coming out of a side hall and heard his name. "What happened?" he asked the agitated group. They all answered at once. Tuck waited, a patient smile on his lips.

"If you are still alive, doctor," he said when things settled a little, "will you please tell me what set all these birdies a-twitter?"

The women laughed, but not too gaily. "Let Dr. Moore tell me," said Tuck.

"He thought he was talking to you," said Dr. Moore.

"Vashon?"

"Yes. And I wish it had been you."

"Well, if he was threatening your life, I don't blame you," said Tucker, leaning over the desk to select a chocolate from a box of candy given to the nurses by some grateful patient.

"I meant," Don told him patiently, "he has not been exactly ready to talk to *any* doctor."

"No, he hasn't," said Tuck. "And he threatened you, or me, or any doctor who would operate on his son."

"That's what he did, sir."

"Well, this whole thing has driven the man crazy."

"And you think that's good?"

"Not good. But it happens."

"Sure does," said the Floor Head. "Remember Dr. Heyd?" Most of them did remember Dr. Heyd, and those who did not were quickly enlightened. Tuck listened, ate another piece of candy, and selected one for Dr. Moore. "Got to keep your energy up," he murmured.

"Dr. Heyd," began Mrs. Adams, "was a sweet old thing . . ."

"Fine surgeon," said someone else, "working older than most doctors will."

"But still very, very sharp," said the Head. "And one day an angry patient came into the office — Heyd was a thoracic surgeon — locked the door and demanded to see the x-rays that had been taken of his chest. Heyd happened to have them and said they showed no difficulties, that was why the hospital had not admitted the patient. But this guy got mad — I never did know why. Maybe he thought there *was* something wrong and they just wouldn't take him in. Anyway, he pulled out a long, sharp knife and began to slash at Dr. Heyd. Dr. Heyd raised his hand to protect his throat, and the guy cut Heyd's index finger clear off."

"Was there ever blood!" contributed another nurse.

"Well, he lost two pints at least. They found him in the hall outside his office, and it took eight surgeons four hours . . ."

"Five, Laura," said Dr. Fairbairn.

"All right, five hours."

"Five surgeons, two hours."

"Well, O.K. But he's never been able to do surgery since, though he still says those doctors did a marvelous job on his tendons. And anyway, doctor, it shows threats can be something to look out for."

"Oh, I'll look out for this one. And so will Moore. Do you girls think we really look alike?"

"Don't answer that," Dr. Moore advised them. "Could I speak to you, Tuck?"

"Sure," said the Chief. "Thanks for the candy, girls. And don't worry. I've been threatened before."

His long stride made it seem that he hurried after his assistant. "I am sorry that happened," he said.

"So am I," said Don. "It should make the surgery harder for you to do."

"Oh, yes. The father's opposition. And then it is always hard enough, to cut off a child's leg."

As things evolved, the surgery on Bob Vashon was delayed for twenty-four hours. Because of the tremor in the child's hand,

Tuck wanted a heart evaluation done, though, he agreed, whatever the report, the surgery had to be performed.

The nurses on the floor were sure that the delay was due to the threat made on Sunday. One of them asked Dr. Moore if that was not the reason, and his answer — "No, it was not!" — was firm enough to convince them, but not entirely.

On Monday evening, Dr. Fairbairn showed up on Surgical just about supper time. He proffered his usual joke, something about two capons and a flock of chickens. "That's funny," he instructed his listeners.

"Yes, doctor," said one of the nurses.

"O.K., O.K.," he said. "I'll tell it to Amscar."

"And the pesky thing will probably laugh," an orderly told him.

"Don't you like robots?" Dr. Fairbairn asked innocently.

The orderly and the nurses regarded the six-foot-tall automatic car which served meals, brought linens, carried away waste from all the floors of the hospital. It moved on tracks from basement to sixth floor; it was programmed to enter and leave elevators at the proper floors. It saved the hospital thousands of dollars, and eliminated dozens of personnel.

"You know," Tuck told the group at the Station, "I came in from the garage yesterday morning and said, 'Excuse me,' to one of the damn things that was barreling toward me."

"Did it answer?"

"No, but I'll bet it would laugh at my joke."

But the Amscar had already gone into the elevator with its load of trays and used dishes, and Tuck went down toward Bob Vashon's room.

"Pardon me, Dr. Fairbairn," said a man who had been using the pay telephone and now held his hand out to stop the doctor. "Would you answer a question for me?"

A reporter. Tuck frowned.

"Would you tell me briefly, doctor," said the man who was short, stout, and bearded. "How do you feel about doing this court-ordered surgery on Stowe Vashon's son?"

"A brief answer, eh?" said Tuck. "Well, here it is. No, I won't tell you." He went swiftly around the man, and on down the hall.

He turned into Bob's room, and closed the door behind him. "You may take a break if you like," said the doctor to the nurse who, at his entrance, rose from her chair.

Bob was in bed, but he wore his blue robe and he had his puppets on the pillow beside him. He managed a smile for Tuck, who was looking at the chart.

"They didn't give you much supper, did they?" he asked the boy.

"That's 'cause I'm pre — pre-op — well, pre-something."

"Pre-operative?" said Tuck. "They use some terrible words in this hospital."

"I like big words, even when I don't know what they mean," said the child. "Will you tell me . . . ?"

Tuck bent over him with his stethoscope. "Don't talk for a minute, Bob," he said. "Please?"

The boy clamped his lips together, and waited.

"Now!" said the tall man. "What was it?"

Bob's big eyes — Carrie's eyes, and Megan's — looked up at his friend. "Are you going to cut off my leg?" he asked.

These times, a doctor had to train his muscles like an athlete. Now Tucker Fairbairn sat down in the chair beside the high bed. "Have you tried asking your mother that?" he asked quietly.

"She wouldn't tell me. But I heard it on the radio."

Damn. Damn. Damn! The doctor reached

for the hands of this very ill, and intelligent, child. "Doctoring is a hard business, Bob," he said slowly. "People keep getting sick, or hurt, and somebody has to learn how to make them feel better, or get well. You understand that?"

"Yes. Like my leg hurting."

"Like that, yes. And it has hurt, I know." The small red head nodded up and down.

"We don't want that hurt to go on, do we?"

Now the head moved from side to side.

"We don't want the other leg to hurt, or your arm. So we find out what's made this one hurt." He moved his big, warm hand to rest on Bob's knee. "And we decide we could stop that hurt by removing the leg that has the sickness."

"The 'fection," Bob contributed. "And you'll cut it off." He sat up straight and looked at the leg in question. "I've had it a long time," he told the doctor.

"Yes, you have," said Tuck. "It's been a good friend until it got sick."

"I'll have to ride in a wheel chair, won't I?" said Bob.

"Yes. For a time."

"Then I could use scrutches."

"And get a new leg . . ."

"Like the man in *Treasure Island*?"

"Oh, we have better ones than that kind, Bob! You'll learn to do all sorts of things with the legs they have now. Walk, and ride a bicycle . . . Why, I know a man who learned to pole-vault with just one leg. Do you know what pole vaulting is?"

Bob did know. He made gestures, and told Tuck that he knew, even as he was thoughtfully considering that feat. "Yes," he said slowly, "I think I could learn to do things like that, when I'm old enough. I could be a doctor, too, like you are. Couldn't I?"

"Oh, sure. Easy."

"And a lawyer like my Dad if I wanted to."

"He'd like that."

"And could maybe I have also a leg like the man in *Treasure Island*?"

"A peg leg? Sure you could. You could use it on Sundays."

That made Bob giggle, and they talked a little more. The nurse came back and Tuck took the pill and the glass of water from her, gave both to Bob. He sat down again and waited until the boy drifted off to sleep.

Then he went out into the hall. *Doctoring was hard business.* Visiting hour was over, lights were being turned off. All along the hall, shadows formed themselves between the pools of soft illumination.

At the far end of the corridor there was a woman, the light burnishing her hair. He hurried his step. It was Carrie and he would have a word or two with her; maybe they could go somewhere . . .

She was talking to some man, probably Don Moore. Earlier Tuck had seen him here on the floor. Dr. Moore had been just about as much concerned with Bob's surgery as had Tuck. Don had two small children of his own. The operation was to be done before a class, and that involved a few special arrangements. Microphones, TV camera — all sorts of things. He —

Tuck braked his step abruptly. The man down the hall was not Dr. Moore; it was Stowe Vashon. Tuck could see his red hair as he bent his head toward Carrie, and — by glory! the man was kissing her! And she had her arm around his neck! Well — *by glory!* Of course, it could be —

But it was *not* a comforting sort of kiss, it was not a sisterly embrace for the father of the child who . . . Stowe was doing the kissing! He definitely was! Of course Carrie was not fighting him off. But neither of them . . .

Tuck stood where he was, and beat his fists together. He was damned mad. He certainly was! Whatever was going on, Carrie had no business . . .

But Stowe sure did. Yes, indeed. This sort of thing was probably what the guy had had in mind when he threatened Tucker Fairbairn! He had said he would get even, that he would make the surgeon sorry. And if this was his method, it had reached its target. No gun fired at close range would have brought these results. Well, Tuck could show that man a thing or two, he could tell him — he could be the one to threaten . . .

Stowe and Carrie were no longer at the end of the hall. The floor shone clean and empty. And Tuck could bend over the drinking fountain, trying to get control of himself. What kind of row had he been ready to make there in the hospital corridor, what sort of fight . . . ?

He unclenched his fists and made every effort to loosen his muscles, to clear his brain. He was still angry. To have to control himself made him as mad as hell! A fellow should be able to shout, and flail his fists, and — and —

Tuck turned and went back as far as the nearest elevator. But of course he must change his clothes, and sign out — check the night orders. Which he did, tight-lipped and stern. Those who watched him thought tomorrow's ordeal was weighing on him. It was not. He did not relish what he would have to do, but there was no choice, and he would see the thing through. But Stowe — and Carrie — that was another thing!

Now he could step into the elevator, push buttons, stride across the chilly garage to his car, get into it, and start the engine. Automatically he locked doors, waited for clearance — and drove away. Out into the open streets, out on the highway, well lighted here in the city, and pretty well lighted until the turnoff into his feeder road, and not lighted at all when he reached the gravel and tar of his own property. There his headlights made a tunnel between the trees. A rabbit scuttled, terrified, across the roadway. And there was his house, a light at the front door, a lamp glowing in his living room. An electric eye precaution to give the appearance of occupancy. He slid his car into the shelter, and went inside — not that he wanted anything there. He still had quite a mood to get rid of, and sitting before an open fire would not do it.

But he went in, checking on the place, the big mirror which doubled the living room; he ran his fingertips along the mantel. And as he watched that hand, he saw and felt his fist clench; again it lifted to pound against the wood, but he could not hurt that hand, and he wished he could stop thinking. It got a man looking at things he would much rather not see. Slowly he relaxed his hand again, and smoothed the palm along the silky wood. He himself had planed and rubbed and waxed the thick mantel board until it glowed with all the sunshine of its growth in the woods, and satisfied the eye with the warmth of the fire it sheltered on his hearth.

He looked around the room, picked up one of the coffee mugs from the low table, set it down again. He got warmer gloves and his knitted cap from the closet beside the front door, checked to be sure he had his keys firmly in his jacket pocket, and he went outside.

The air was crisply cold but there was only a light wind. A bright new moon shone directly overhead, the ground under his feet crackled with frost.

And he walked. He knew the paths well, though perhaps he should have brought a flashlight. The moon was still crescent but its light reflected from the water of the lake, and Tuck would not stay out long, nor go far. For the thousandth time, he wished he had a dog for company. But a dog must be left alone all day, penned or tied. Tuck would not treat any animal so. But he still wished . . .

His foot caught on a fallen branch and he swore a little, bent, lifted the thing and threw it into the lake. He was still angry. Of course he was.

He knew that Stowe could not have set up the tender little scene there under the exit light at the end of the long hall. But he could take advantage of an opportunity. He sure could and did that. He had probably come to the hospital, maybe planning to look in on Bob. He had learned that the doctor was with the boy, and had gone down to the room where Megan would spend the night. Carrie had been with Megan, and was probably starting for home. Meeting her, as Stowe had talked to her, he had seen Tuck, the doctor in white, coming toward them, and had taken advantage of the opportunity . . .

That he had done! He most certainly had! And Tuck was mad about the whole thing. He guessed he couldn't, under the circumstances, expect Carrie to slap her brother-in-law, but what about that arm around his neck? What about it?

This path led along the lake edge, and little waves lifted and splashed against the rocks; the tall trees blew in the wind, creaking and rubbing their branches together. In the darkness, nature was talking to him, and he usually listened to what it had to say. Tonight he should listen. But there was that damn thinking still! He might as well get it done, and be able to put it out of his head.

So, in his mind and memory, he looked again at the small, brief scene he had witnessed. There was the circle of light, and Carrie in a skirt and white blouse, talking to a shadowy man. He had moved into the light, had drawn her to him and bent his head. One of her arms had gone up, and around his neck . . .

And Tucker Fairbairn was angry. At Vashon, of course, though not entirely for kissing Carrie. Tonight he must be in a highly emotional state.

But there was Carrie herself. She should be Tuck's, and only Tuck's, his alone to kiss that way.

That way. The way — ten years ago — Tucker had seen the same Stowe Vashon, in wedding frock coat and Ascot tie, embrace and kiss a young girl.

Then Tuck had wondered if Vashon might have married the sister of the girl he really loved. Now — was that man ready to move in again? Had he been moving that way before tonight?

Tuck's foot told him that he had reached the point of land that jutted out into the lake. A bed of shale rock, flat chips and stones, kept down the scrub growth here. It was a good place for a picnic, or for fishing. From this point sometimes Tuck swam in the lake. Tonight he stood there thinking, and trying not to think. His knees bent and his hand caught up a half dozen of the white flat stones. He took them one by one in his fingers, and drew back his arm, then threw the rock, underhand, watching it skip and skip again across the moonpath of the water. He gathered another handful of rocks, and threw them . . .

And he thought . . .

That he did not like the idea which had unwillingly come into his head. If Stowe Vashon had used to be in love with Carrie — even when she had been only seventeen — and things had — not — worked out — for the two — of them . . . For Stowe, which they certainly had not!

Just as they would not work out now, when Carrie was wearing Tuck's ring. She had not lightly accepted that ring.

But Stowe Vashon, that strange man — was it possible that the creature he seemed to be was opposing surgery on his son, had opposed it from the first, to use that means to strike out at Carrie, through Tuck, because he knew that he had finally lost the girl completely? He knew what her ring meant to Carrie, he knew that she would indeed marry Tuck very soon — just as he knew that he loved a girl he could not ever have. In the past, or in the future . . .

So Tucker Fairbairn must stand on the edge of a cold lake, on a cold night, and think about this dreadful idea. He must watch the little waves wash up to his feet, dissolve, and come up again, and again, repeating themselves even as his thoughts repeated, going round and round. Stowe had loved Carrie, he had lost her, and now he wanted another man to lose her. If he could manage that . . .

Tucker shivered and turned back toward his house. It was indeed a dreadful idea, and with it surging and boiling in his mind, how could he go on and do the surgery on Stowe's son twelve hours from now? Could he do it? Had he the right to do it?

Not because of the mental and emotional turmoil, but because of the close relationship which he found himself in with the patient's family. His deep love for Carrie — Stowe's possible jealousy, and his certain fear . . .

But this surgery was Tuck's specialty. He

had devoted fifteen years of his life to studying just such problems, learning tediously to detect, evaluate, and solve them through treatment and surgery. His fingers were skilled, his eyes, his mind trained. Without vanity, he knew that he was considered a master in the subject of bone diseases and the surgery they required. It was a classic example of his own techniques which his surgery would employ the next morning.

There were other considerations. Megan, the boy's mother, had gone through pure hell to give her son this one chance the boy had.

And Bob himself — wanting a peg leg as substitute for the one he must lose, ready to accept the disaster of disease and look forward to a future which Tuck had offered him, and in all likelihood would provide.

So — yes. Tuck, Dr. Fairbairn, must operate the next morning. There would be no more thinking on that point.

He had by then reached his own clearing. His boots crunched on the gravel of his own driveway. He unlocked the door and went inside, up the stairs to his bedroom where he undressed, showered, and got into his bed, without turning on any more light than the small copper lamp that would turn itself off around midnight. He would not read. With decisions made, he would sleep.

Seven

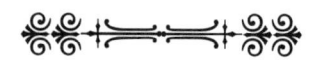

And slept so soundly that the alarm must waken him, only five minutes before the surgery resident phoned him to remind him of the day's schedule. Tuck thanked him, yawned, and reached for the light. He must get up, fix something for his breakfast, and get to the hospital. He peered at the weather through the triangle of the front window; there was fog — mist rising from the lake. But no snow had fallen during the night, nor any of that horror, freezing rain. Daylight was coming reluctantly, — and much in the same mood, Tuck went, barefooted, across to the bathroom, turned on the light, shucked out of his pajamas, and faced himself in the mirror above the basin. He raised his hand to brush back his hair, and stopped short. Some trick of light made the back of his hand seem to be —

He looked at it directly. He frowned, and looked at the other hand, at his forearms. He stepped back so that the mirror showed him his body to the waist.

And he yelled in disbelief. This could not be! But there it was. A *rash!* In splotches of red welts and watery blisters on his body, the same thing on his arms — and his hands. *His hands!* The bathroom was white-lighted, but he took himself to the window of the bedroom and looked at his hands in the gray daylight there. Fluorescent lighting, his thoughts reminded him, gave strange images. Sometimes.

Not that morning. The rash was there. Red, angry welts, and blistery ones. If he rubbed one, there was itching.

Oh, gee, pops! What *was* this? What was fate doing to him now? Never in his life had this happened to him! Even as an adolescent, his acne stage had been mild and brief. He had skin like tanned leather, and he — He showered and pulled on some clothes, glad to cover his body, to conceal as much of his offensive skin as possible. He swore aloud, and he swore inwardly.

He did not feel like breakfast, but he had last eaten at five the night before. Tennant's report had outlined a busy day. And of course there was Bob's surgery . . .

Swearing still, he plugged in the coffee pot, put strips of bacon in a pan, poured cereal into a bowl. And all the time he looked at his hands. They were big hands, the fingers long and blunt-ended, scrubbed and scrubbed and scrubbed to pink, soft flesh, with squared-off nails as clean as porcelain. Black hair thinly masked the backs of his hands and fingers. But nothing hid the rash. Was it getting worse? Oh, he imagined that!

He sat down at the table, poured milk on the cereal, and dug his sharp spoon into the grapefruit. And he looked at his hands.

He had thought that every complication had risen to foul up Bob's case. He had not counted on his own body to interfere. It never had before. He seldom had colds, he almost never had a digestive upset — he could always schedule surgery, confident that he would perform it on schedule.

But not today. Not with blisters and lesions all over his dadblasted hands and body! Would it disappear as quickly as it had come? If it were due to nerves, it might. But *nerves!* He would not consider such a thing! Tuck Fairbairn had no nerves. Not in that sense.

Naw, this had to be an allergic reaction to something he had eaten or contacted. Maybe from the water of the lake; there was that branch he had handled, picking it up and throwing it out into the water.

It could have been covered with lichen. There were those rocks he had skipped the night before . . .

Let him think! It could be an infection from someone he had examined. Stirling was always talking about the colds the kids handed on to him. What patients, lately — Let him *think!* He got all kinds . . . He took precautions, of course. But —

Frowning, and talking to himself, he ate his breakfast, leaving things for Rose, the woman who came in for an hour or two each morning. He went upstairs and examined himself again in the mirror. And he remembered, from his general-intern days, the old people who suffered from shingles. Herpes of all sorts. They did suffer, and they told the doctor it had to be due to nerves. Worry over finances, over family matters . . .

But Tuck had no "worries." Of course he didn't need 'em if some patient had given these hateful blisters to the doctor intent on helping him. This was a sobering thought. If his rash stayed with him, he could not possibly operate. And in Bob Vashon's case, to operate was imperative. Physically, any further delay was dangerous, mentally his family could not accept delay. Nor would Bob, or his doctor . . .

He pulled on a cotton shirt; wool would only irritate the rash. He went downstairs again and shrugged into a fleece-lined jacket . . . and went back to the idea of nerve-caused rashes. Certainly, for the past couple of weeks, he had had problems. Last night, Stowe and Carrie had stirred every nerve-end in his body. He was disgusted even to consider this possibility. Surely he was too old, too experienced, to let an hour or so of anger make him break out like a jittery teenager! But still he must recognize this solution as the best one among those he had considered. It disgusted him, that a big lug like himself . . .

He got behind his car wheel, absent-mindedly scratching the back of his right hand with his left. Hey! He'd better not do *that!* He had better remember the rash, and consider it in as detached a manner as possible.

He backed out of the car shelter. He drove down his lane and turned into the larger road. There were some joggers even on this chill gray morning. All around him, things were normal. The small truck he always passed, the joggers, and that fool lawyer, a judge or something, on his three-wheeled bike. Last summer this same chap, a rotund fifty-five or so, had used to ride a light motor bike. One morning Tuck had come upon him in the ditch. Scrabbling about in the weeds. His front wheel had struck a rock and pitched him off, his false teeth had jarred loose and out — cracking the upper plate — it was for part of that plate that the jurist hunted. Tuck had helped, unable to restrain his laughter at the picture the man drew of trying to conduct court without any teeth. Now, converted to a three-wheeler, would this same man laugh at Tuck's predicament? Probably not.

Nor did Tuck. He certainly did not!

He drove steadily on to the city, watching his hands. He reached the hospital, parked his car, and told his usual joke to the attendant.

"I know a couple who got married because it was easier to park one car than two."

The man laughed obligingly, and pointed to Carrie's car which stood in the next row. "Won't be long now, will it, Doc?" he asked, leering a bit.

"I hope not," said Tuck, already halfway to the elevator. He must push that foot surgery on some other doctor while he handled his damned rash.

But Bob . . . Oh, damn, damn, *damn!*

The surgical floor was in its usual bustle.

With two o.r.'s open — and the nurses at the desk in a huddle over something — the teams were assembling. Tuck took his coat to his office, and looked at his hands again. He would have to talk to someone about that. Moore might have a bright idea . . .

Out at the desk, the nurses were indeed in a twitter. That redheaded fellow had just gone down the hall — the one who had threatened Dr. Moore. He was little Bob's father. Oh, not really!

He should wait downstairs. Get someone to take him down. Yeah, and get him to stay!

"And maybe we can get to work," said the Floor Head tartly. "Who's working for Carrie in o.r.?"

Carrie was to wait downstairs too, said Mrs. Adams. "Has Dr. Fairbairn shown up?"

"He's in his office."

The Floor Head nodded, and gathered up some papers, ready to hurry down there. Everyone hurried. Bells rang, voices rose, in spite of efforts to keep things calm. Each one had to talk to someone. So voices raised the decibel count. Carts went along, and traffic jams were inevitable.

Tuck followed the Floor Head out of his office; he had put on white ducks and a jacket. They were talking earnestly to each other, and the other nurses became concerned. Something must have happened. . . .

Tuck went behind the counter and sat down at the chart desk. "Will someone put in a call for Junior Steinbach?" he asked, reading Bob's chart. "He will be at home."

Dr. Steinbach was the staff dermatologist.

"He has a rash . . ." murmured the Floor Head.

At that announcement, things did go into a twitter. Tuck heard it; he leaned back in the creaking chair, and showed his hands, pushing up his sleeves. "Delayed adolescence," he told Dr. Tennant, who did not laugh.

"What are you going to do?" asked that young doctor. "Does Moore know?"

"I didn't know myself until two hours ago," said Tuck.

"But, doctor . . ."

Tuck nodded, and accepted the phone which Mrs. Adams held toward him. Everyone at the desk, and a growing number from the hall, stopped to listen. Mrs. Adams put her finger to her lips, and heads nodded. They wouldn't talk about it. But, for heaven's sake . . .

Everyone listened. The bustling traffic in

the hall practically came to a standstill.

"Hello, Junior!" said Tuck firmly. "Fairbairn here."

"Sure I'm at the hospital. Only fellas like you had the brains to go into dermatology. No 8 A.M. surgery for you! Well, listen to what I have to say and you can go back to bed. Yeah, seems I do have a problem."

And for five minutes, scarcely interrupted, he told about the rash. No. No history of it. No allergy that he knew of. He described the red welts, the blisters — the itching on contact. Sure it was a hell of a thing. Tuck had surgery at eight and at ten. The eight o'clock could be transferred, the ten, no. He had hoped Steinbach . . .

"I can't, over the telephone, Tuck."

"Could you possibly . . . ?"

"Well, yes, I suppose so. If you think it's important."

Tuck explained the importance so vividly that the people in the station giggled. He ended by advising Dr. Steinbach to go back to bed. "I'll see if I can find me another doctor."

He gave the phone back and told Mrs. Adams that he was going to see Dr. Webb.

Before she could make any reply, he was striding down the hall. He found that he was angry again. But it was the job of the

Chief of Medical Services to solve these problems.

He had reached Bob's room before he remembered that he must pass it. And of course he glanced in. The child was being prepared; a cap was on his shining head, and Megan was standing beside his bed, holding the blue robe, folded neatly over her arm.

Megan was a little pale, but doing a masterly job of seeming calm to the child. Bob was accepting everything being done to him as part of an adventure. He was talking, and occasionally he sought to divert his mother or the nurse. Tuck smiled a little and started on, but Carrie saw the big, white-clad man and came around the door to speak softly to him, to detain him. In spite of her wishes to help in o.r., or at least to be there, she was in mufti, a light rose blouse, an almost dark-red skirt. Her hair was tied back with a flat rose-colored bow.

"Tuck?" she called. "Did you want something?" Then she saw his face. "Oh!" she breathed. "Is something wrong?"

He held out his hands for her to see, and moved to where the light was even brighter.

She looked at his hands, she touched his fingertip lightly, she looked up into his face. Shocked, and frightened. "What happened?" she asked.

He shook his head. "Damned if I know. Got up this morning — there it was. On my arms and body, too."

"Does it hurt?"

"Itches, some. I guess I could make it hurt. The thing is, puddin', I probably can't operate this morning."

She frowned and glanced back toward Bob's room. "But you have to!" she said softly, fiercely.

"I know I have to, but until we know about this confounded stuff — I'm on my way now to see Webb."

The Chief of Medical Services.

"Your gloves would cover it."

He smiled at her, and she began to cry. "Hey!" he cried. "That won't help."

She sniffed. "It might help me. I just know you have to take care of Bob."

"I have two scheduled for this morning." He glanced at his watch. "Now, I'd better hurry. If the Chief agrees with you, and says I can operate, I'll be back here, running. Meanwhile, don't worry."

"You're worried."

"Somewhat, yes. But it isn't doing me any good. And we both can be sure that Bob will be taken care of."

He pressed Carrie's arm, touched her cheek with his finger, and went on down the hall. In Dr. Webb's office, he talked for a brief time, and then waited while the Chief assembled the entire surgical staff of Skull and Bones. They came in, *stat,* some still in street clothes, some in white, three in green. Dr. Moore was one of those. He went directly over to Tuck and demanded to see his hands. Tuck showed him, he showed them all. He stood up, pulled up his jumper to show his torso, flat-bellied, leanly muscled — and streaked with welts and blisters.

"Pretty, pretty," said one man.

Tuck's lips drew in grimly. "This just isn't any surgery," he reminded the group.

Someone made a joke, which Tuck resented. Dr. Webb tapped his eyeglasses against his telephone. "Gentlemen!" he said mildly. "This is, as Tuck says, important. It is urgent. This is, as Tuck says, a special sort of case, because of the court order."

"Was that specifically for Fairbairn to operate?" asked one of the older doctors.

Everyone looked at Tuck. He shook his head. "My name was mentioned, and the type of surgery given in detail, but no — no, I was not specified. Though" — he swung his arms — "I sure as hell expected to do it. And so does the family."

For a short time, everyone spoke at once.

They expressed sympathy for Tuck, and meant it. Each and every one suggested reasons for the appearance of the rash. They settled down to calling it hives. They offered suggestions for treatment. Had Tuck talked to Steinbach? What had Junior said? To a man they understood Fairbairn's dilemma. They all were concerned.

"Can't you postpone things." asked one doctor, as if this was an inspired solution.

"The toe amputation could be postponed," Tuck agreed. "But the boy's knee disarticutation — no, definitely not.

"We've delayed it to the limit of safety," he explained, "because of the father's resistance, his reluctance to have the child's leg amputated. That's why I asked for the court order, and got it."

"Besides . . ." He paused, thinking, then lifted his head. "Besides," he said, "psychologically, a delay of any surgery is always bad. Especially for a child."

"Does he know what . . . ?"

"Yes, he does. He has been told."

There was a silence.

"It's Billings' day off," said a graft man. "He could come in — not foul up everybody's schedule."

Tuck swung on him. "The devil with your schedules!" he shouted. "I won't have Billings —" He broke off and went toward the door. "Let me know what you decide," he said in a muffled tone.

"Tuck," said the Chief. "Wait!"

Tuck stopped and returned, as of course he must return. The decision lay with Dr. Webb, where it had begun. He was Chief of Medical Services. But Billings . . .

He went to stand beside Dr. Moore. *Billings,* he growled. A capable surgeon, but both men were remembering the day, not too long ago, when Billings had called in sick, and dumped his cases on Tuck and his assistant. Today — well, it was Billings' day off! He was free to putter around that awful house of his. He bragged that the landscaping had all been done by him personally. The terrace descended in steps down from the house, there were Chinese-sort-of stone lanterns, and walks of some blue stuff that shone like glass. Topiary trees . . .

"I'd rather have dope-eaters move into the neighborhood," had been Tuck's first comment on that house. He had felt obliged to go to the housewarming. And had found a clear Lucite toilet seat embedded with coins of all denominations.

Billings was a capable surgeon, but he had the taste of a billy goat. "Got to get him off my staff," Tuck had said in Moore's ear.

The Chief cleared his throat, and he was looking at the semicircle of surgeons who faced him.

"I think, Tuck," he said quietly, "that you should let Dr. Moore do the surgery for you. I think we will both agree that he is capable." Tuck's head nodded. "You can't scrub, I fear," the Chief continued, "but you should be ready to stand by, should there be any complications."

Tuck nodded. "There probably won't be," he said quietly.

"I agree," said the Chief. "I'll have Steinbach come in and give you a shot of something."

"Will that help?" asked the resident, Tennant.

Dr. Webb smiled at him. "I feel *I* must do something," he explained to the young doctor.

"Yes, sir," said Tennant.

"Are you in agreement, Dr. Moore?" asked the Chief.

Dr. Moore had started for the door. "Sir?" he asked, turning. "Oh, yes, sir. Of course I'll do whatever I can. And first of all, I'll stand by Tuck when Steinbach gets here with his shot."

The meeting broke up with the men all

laughing at Tuck's face. But even he laughed by the time he caught up with his assistant.

"We might as well do the toe," he growled in Don's ear.

"I'm sorry as hell about this, Tuck."

Tuck growled again.

Up on the floor, preparations were going ahead full blast. The two tall men turned into the locker room and changed into scrub suits, caps, masks. Dr. Tennant joined them. No one was inclined to talk.

"I'm as nervous as a bride," Dr. Moore said once.

Tuck's retort was unprintable. They moved to scrub. There, when Dr. Fairbairn stood against the wall instead of going to the basin, the team learned of the substitution. "I'll do a dress rehearsal on the first case," Dr. Moore told them. "Hey. Tuck! Are we still doing the A/K before a class?"

"Why not?" asked Dr., Fairbairn. The scrub nurse was offering him gloves and a towel in which to enfold his hands.

They did the "toe," and moved to the second o.r. Bob already lay upon the table there, asleep. Tuck stayed at Moore's shoulder. "I am *sorry* to do this to you, Don," he again attempted an apology.

"... what an assistant is for," said Dr. Moore.

"Yes, of course it is."

The team was ready, all eyes alert. Tuck made his usual survey. The only change was that he stayed at Moore's shoulder when surgery would begin. For three years Tucker had trained Moore. The slightly younger man had even learned Fairbairn's little mannerisms. He glanced up at the circling benches of students. "Good morning, gentlemen," he said, his voice muffled behind the plastic cup-like mask. "Dr. Tennant will lecture."

And they were ready to begin. Tuck did not need to speak. Dr. Moore was doing everything as he would have done it. The pediatric surgeon stood across from Don, ready should he be needed.

Outside, out in the hall, tension rose like mist. Carrie was staying with Megan, though she did so want to observe the surgery. She had accepted Tuck's ruling that she could not work that morning, but there was an overlook where she might have watched. But she did stay with Megan. "We should go downstairs," she said once, and then again.

"Where is Stowe?"

"He was taken down there an hour ago."

"Do you think he would want me to be with him?"

"I don't know, Megan. I haven't much understood his behavior in this."

"He's so frightened . . . Men get stubborn or angry when they are frightened."

"I suppose some of them do. Let's go downstairs. That's where we are supposed to be. They'll tell us when it is over."

Megan consented, but as they waited for the elevator, Carrie was sure she saw Stowe come out of the cross hall, and then duck back out of sight. She would not mention this strange behavior to her sister, who was upset enough. They went downstairs to the waiting room provided for families of surgical cases.

Meanwhile, in o.r., work proceeded. Tuck stood close enough to the surgeon's shoulder that Don Moore could feel the warmth of his body. But the substitute doctor understood what the Chief was going through. If his rash was due to nerves he must now be just one big red welt!

"Clamp," he said quietly. Dr. Tennant's voice was relaying the procedure to the observers; he was doing a good job. The room was quiet, as such things went. There were the regular noises, and the lecturer's voice this morning. The instruments on the tiled walls clicked and pinged, there were other familiar hisses and hums. The anaesthetist regularly gave his readings.

Tuck stood as tall and as stiff as a tree trunk, but he was "doing" each thing himself; his hands filled the gloves Moore had worn when he opened the amp kit and arranged the gleaming instruments into neat rows, ties and sutures tucked under a sterile towel so that they could be drawn out one by one. He, as a surgeon, always did this for himself, and so Moore had learned.

Tennant, the resident, positioned their small patient and began to give a spinal under the eye of the anaesthesiologist.

Bob moaned softly. The scrub nurse, the one who was replacing Carrie, scrubbed the leg down and she and Moore draped. He looked up at Tuck, who, five inches above the child, traced with his gloved finger the route of the below-knee incision.

"You are going to make a cut to give you long anterior and short posterior flaps," he said. Moore knew this. But to say it was the only way in which Tuck could share this critical surgery. Now he glanced at Tennant, who said to the observers, "This is done so that when it heals, the boy can walk on skin and the scar behind the skin." He glanced at Dr. Moore, handed him the knife, then began to slap snaps to clamp the bleeders as fast as the surgeon cut through them. Together, under Tuck's watchful eye, they worked until there were ten or a dozen snaps running through the incision, then they paused to tie off the bleeders and remove the snaps.

Tuck glanced up at the overhead light, then back at Moore's hands and Tennant's. "Aren't you cutting too low?" he said. "You should want the linea aspera up higher, else you could push the periosteum up to where it will re-ossify, and produce a spur."

Moore cut again, a thread higher. Tuck's nerves were really showing! he thought, else he would not delay the amputation.

"Will you get me some absolute alcohol?" he asked the circulating. Then *her* nerves showed. "What do you need it for?" she asked.

"To inject the nerve," said Tuck, with a show of patience.

Tennant had found the femoral artery and tied it off. The circulating brought the alcohol, Moore located the sciatic nerve, crushed it high, ligated it, and injected the alcohol.

"Bone wax, please," asked Dr. Moore.

Tennant held the saw ready.

The electrocardiograph monitor sounded its bleep, bleep; the blips marched across the screen.

"Watch your blood," Tuck told Moore.

"I am watching it," said Don, not taking the saw.

Under the drape, the child's arm began to twitch.

"He's having trouble with the oxygen, doctor," said the anaestheologist.

"B.P.?"

"Almost none, and his heart is arythmic."

"pH?"

"6.9"

"Is the sodium bicarbonate ready?" asked Dr. Fairbairn.

There was a break in the rhythm. Tennant's voice lifted, heads turned to the green glass monster where the heartbeats had been bleeping away. Someone said, "Oh, my God!" and Tucker Fairbairn pushed his way to the table.

". . . arrest!" he shouted unnecessarily. "Get a converter!"

Someone else was yelling, "Code 2!" into the telephone. The team was there and ready.

All eyes went swiftly to the monitor, the yellow lights, each a contraction of the dying heart muscle, bloomed into life with decreasing frequency, the little crests of light appeared as fainter lines with lower peaks until finally, as everyone watched, the blips flattened out.

Tennant began the steady, intermittent pressure on the chest wall with the heel of his hand. "Bicarbonate," said Dr. Moore, his voice breaking.

Bear down.

Lift up.

Bear down.

"Epinephrine?" asked Moore, looking up at Tuck.

The nurse flicked the glass ampule and broke it open. Moore's syringe drank the hormone as he injected it into another leg muscle. He looked up at the clock. "How long?" he asked harshly.

"Four minutes, thirty-two seconds."

"Oh, God," said Dr. Moore.

Tennant continued his rocking, back and forth. Again and again.

"Sir?" he asked to Dr. Fairbairn.

"Five minutes," said Tuck.

"He . . ." Yes, the brain was gone, that long without oxygen.

"Try the bicarb again."

They did try it. And it was no good.

"I'll open," said Tuck harshly.

Dr. Moore held his arm. "It's no use, Tuck."

"But . . ."

The pediatric surgeon pushed his hands away from Bob's body. "I'll do it," he said.

But all they did, all the cardiac team tried, was of no use. Bob's small heart had just stopped — and those who had seen it happen were shocked and disbelieving.

". . . suspected a clot," Tuck muttered.

The scrub nurse was sobbing noisily. Someone roughly told her to shut up. It was Tuck who finally accepted the sheet and drew it over Bob. "He's so little," he said wearily.

"I'll talk to the family," Dr. Moore offered.

"Oh — gee —" Tuck tried to speak. "Tell them . . ."

"I know what to tell them," said Dr. Moore. He patted the surgeon's arm.

"Go with him, doctor," Tuck said to Tennant.

He looked around the room . . . Someone handed him the chart. "10:37." He was told the time of the cardiac arrest. Tuck shook his head. There it was. Robert Vashon, well-nourished male, white, aged 4 . . .

And never to be any older. Never to wear his peg leg, or learn to pole-vault. How would Tuck face Megan and Carrie? What could he expect from Stowe? He himself was so devastated . . .

He went to the door. There would be an autopsy, he reminded the intern, particularly to find that clot, and to assess the bone damage done by the cancer. He went through to scrub, dropped his gloves and mask, picked up his Gokey brush, then hurled it at the wall. He went on to Bob's empty room. He saw the blue robe and the puppet Tigger. He smoothed them with his hand. Bob. Dear Bob. He would never learn to walk on scrutches, he would never . . .

Oh, gee, pops! he thought silently. "Oh, gee . . ."

Carrying the robe, he went out into the hall. "Where's Moore?" he asked.

"Did you expect this, doctor?" asked the nurse who was coming in to take care of the room.

"No, I did not!" said Tuck vigorously. Somehow, the routine, even silly, question had snapped him back to reality. He — everyone — was thinking of the child, the bright-haired, clear-voiced child. And of the mother, the father — but especially those co-workers thought of the doctor who did not operate.

★ ★ ★

Out in the hall of Surgical, opposing, disobeying all orders and suggestions that he stay downstairs, Stowe Vashon had been the first to realize that something had happened. That something was wrong. There was a certain alertness on the part of the nurse who answered a telephone, the hushed concern of the people she spoke to. Groups began to form all along the hall . . .

He drew in his breath sharply, and, pushing a Gurney wheeling out of his way, he ran across to the fire stairs; its well doors flapped behind him.

Like a rock tumbling, he ran down the stairs; he burst into the fifth-floor corridor. "Where's my wife?" he shouted at an orderly. "Where . . . ?"

Carrie heard the noise he was making, and came out of the waiting room. Megan followed a few feet behind her. "Please, Stowe . . ." said Carrie warningly.

"What's happened?" asked Megan, her face like clay.

The Floor Nurse came toward the group. "Miss Reynolds . . ." she protested.

"I know, I know," said Carrie. "He's upset —"

The Floor Head reached for the telephone. Carrie put her hand on Stowe's arm.

He stood like a man of wood, stiff, hurt, protesting. His lips were drawn into a thin, tight line. His eyes were like green marbles.

He pushed Carrie's hand away. "What the hell is going *on?*" he cried.

Carrie turned to meet the approaching Floor Head, they spoke together for a minute, then Carrie returned. She led Megan back to the waiting room, Stowe followed them. And Carrie, biting her lips for control, told them. "He collapsed," she said. "His heart did. And" — she spread her hands — "he died. He — he was a very sick little boy, you know."

"And Fairbairn had to operate on him," said Stowe savagely.

"No," said Carrie. "No, he did not operate."

Stowe leaned toward her. "I don't believe you," he spat the words into her face. Hatred held the man like thin steel.

Carrie went around him and closed the door into the hall. "Now, see here, Stowe," she attempted.

She was still trying to comfort Megan, and restrain Stowe, when the door opened, and Dr. Webb came in, his face grave, his manner quiet. He was an older man, dignified, sure of himself. They all turned to him and listened to him.

"I am Dr. Webb," he said quietly, his eyes flicking to Carrie then back again to the devastated parents. "Dr. Moore phoned me immediately. I can see that you have been told that the patient collapsed on the table and died."

"He's dead all right," rasped Stowe. "Do we have to talk about it?"

"Yes, I think we do," said Dr. Webb. "This is a terrible thing —"

He tried to talk to them. Megan sat numbly, not weeping, not speaking. Carrie's head was down, and her tears flowed freely. She was crushed; she had never thought . . . Stowe stood over by the window, still wooden-faced and resentful.

Once Megan spoke. She turned to Stowe and said accusingly, "You refused surgery. You wanted Bob just to die."

"He did die," said Stowe.

Dr. Webb sighed and stood up. This was a terrible thing. "The surgery was necessary," he said firmly. "It was progressing well — but the boy's heart stopped, and then of course . . . It simply stopped."

"Fairbairn could have done something . . ." cried Stowe. "If he's so damned wonderful . . ."

"Dr. Fairbairn was right at Dr. Moore's side. The whole surgical team was there, and the cardiac team came in immediately. They all tried to 'do something,' Mr. Vashon. But the boy's heart had stopped, and nothing could be done."

"Nothing *was* done," said Stowe bitterly. Nothing could be said which he would believe. Tucker Fairbairn had killed his son. That he knew.

"I'm sorry, Megan," said Dr. Webb. "Carrie, you should take her home."

"Yes, doctor. Stowe . . . ?"

But Stowe could endure no more. He threw open the door and went out into the hall. "Now it's my turn," he said as he passed Dr. Webb.

He used the stairs again, and at the top of them he met Dr. Moore, who was coming down to speak to Bob's family. He'd given Dr. Webb the fifteen minutes he had asked to have.

"You . . ." Stowe shouted.

Moore backed up. The man was crazed, and he still thought Dr. Moore was Tuck.

Someone screamed, almost everyone ran in one direction or the other. Stowe Vashon ran. The smoking gun still in his hand, he raced down the corridor, shouting, pushing people away, knocking into an i.v. stand, crashing it against the tiled wall.

It was a terrible thing to have happen in

a modern hospital. Even the intern stationed in Recovery came out to see what all the noise was about.

"He just pulled out a gun," said a nurse, "and shot Dr. Moore."

"Why?"

The girl shrugged. "I don't know why. He ran . . ."

And Don Moore leaned against the wall, his left hand clasping his right arm. "He shot me," he said, unbelieving. "He *shot* me."

"Fall down, will you?" said one of the cardiac men who had come into the area only minutes ago to help Bob.

It was only one of the orders being given. That part of surgical was in complete pandemonium. Panic, hysteria, orders were shouted . . .

But the first attention had to be given to Dr. Moore. And by the time this got under way, Stowe Vashon — "that man" — got entirely away. He had vanished.

Hands pointed to the far end of the corridor; he had been running . . .

And Tucker Fairbairn ran that way too. Down the first flight of stairs, where he met Carrie and Megan ready to go home. Tuck told them what had happened. Had Stowe come down here? he asked, ready to take off again in pursuit.

"Let him go!" said Carrie.

Tuck turned back and looked at her in amazement. "But the man has a gun," he said. "Do you think he should be allowed . . . ?" Then he broke off, bent over and searched Carrie's face. Her beloved face. And seeing her, hearing her, he felt that he too knew tragedy.

"This . . ." he said. "A terrible thing has happened, Carrie, my love." And he walked away.

A terrible thing had happened. The child who trusted him was dead. The woman he loved had turned to the defence of another man against him. Even his own confidence in his surgery was shaken. He could have been wrong to insist that Bob . . .

Yes, a terrible thing had happened.

He waited for the elevator to take Carrie and Megan down, then waited for it to take him up again to Surgical.

And even there he must stand to one side and watch Dr. Tennant, the resident, patch Moore's arm. The bullet had gone through the fleshy part of the upper arm, only grazing the bone. But that bullet had been meant for Tuck . . .

He put out his hand to help with the dressing, and, remembering, drew it back. Moore was looking up at him. "How's the itch?" he asked, so normally that it was like a slap to Tuck's threatening panic.

He spread out his fingers and looked at his hands; he pushed up his sleeve. "Better, of course," he said wryly.

"That shot did it," said the resident.

That," Moore agreed, "or the lessening of tension. You really should never have let Vashon stop or bother you, Tuck."

Tuck threw the scissors back on the tray. "Try my shoes on for size," he said gruffly.

Then you'd have to do your own work," said Dr. Moore, wincing as the arm was moved.

"I can," said his Chief, "and will."

Then he extended his hand. "I didn't mean that," he said quickly. He realized that Moore had had his own traumas that morning. He nodded to his friend and assistant, turned on his heel, and left the room.

Carrie, her own heart bleeding, persuaded Megan to let her take her home. No, she could not see Bob now. No, she didn't like hospitals either. They would get his blue robe later, yes, and his toys. For now — So they went home.

Getting out of Carrie's car, Megan looked up at the house as if she had never seen it before, as if she were going into a strange house. Once inside, she stood there, and let Carrie lift her coat from her shoulders. She looked around. She went into the living room with its stone fireplace and golden rug; she moved toward the kitchen; she ran her fingers down one of the spindles of the breakfast bar. Then she turned to the stairs that led up — just six stairs carpeted, the railing of iron painted dull ivory, with touches of faded gold. Having mounted those six steps, her feet turned to the left, to Bob's room. Carrie followed her. Not speaking. Both were remembering, both realizing . . .

Megan turned to look at her sister, then she buried her face in Carrie's shoulder, and sobbed dryly. Carrie comforted her as best she could. Nothing had been said to ease her own pain. What could she think of to say to Bob's mother?

Where was Stowe? This was his task; Megan needed him. And Carrie needed to turn to Tuck, to try to erase the horror from his face, to comfort him if she possibly could.

She found a cloth and dampened it, gently wiped Megan's face. "We'll go downstairs," said the nurse-sister firmly. "No, Megan, we cannot stay up here. I'll get you a glass of milk, and we'll talk."

"About what?" asked Megan angrily. "What can possibly be said?"

"We have things to do," said Carrie. "We must find Stowe."

Megan looked around. "Where is he? And what is there to do?"

"Many things."

Carrie seated her on the couch, drew the draperies against the noonday sun, then went to the kitchen and brought back two small glasses of milk. "Drink it," she said firmly.

Megan looked up at her, then obediently put the glass to her lips. "Tell me what I have to do," she said pitiably, setting the empty glass on the tray.

"Well, you know there are arrangements to be made. A man will come, —"

Their heads turned. Stowe had opened the front door, and now came in. He looked terrible, his hair rumpled, his coat hanging loosely; somewhere he had taken off his tie. His face was drawn, and blotched with color. Red spots under his eyes, in the hollows of his cheeks.

Megan rose to go to him. He moved away. "I didn't think you would be here," he mumbled.

"Where else would we go?" asked Carrie.

He swung on her. "Shut up, will you?" he asked.

"Someone has to help Megan," she said calmly. "There are arrangements to be made . . ."

"What arrangements?" he rasped. "Didn't you make enough of those when you and your boy friend took over my son?"

There would be no reasoning with this crazed man. He pushed past Megan, went to the tray on the counter and poured Scotch into a glass.

"A man is coming," said Carrie quietly.

Stowe swung on her, the liquor sloshing over his hand, which he put to his lips. "No reporters!" he shouted.

"Of course not," said Carrie, still in that firm, quiet voice. "But there are things to decide. This man will know what those things are."

"There's to be no funeral!" said Stowe.

"There need not be, if that is what you and Megan decide. But there must be a burial. This man will care for that. You must talk to him."

"Not me," said Stove. "You can care for these grisly matters if you think you must. I —"

"They are necessary, but not grisly," said Carrie.

'No, they are not." Unexpectedly, Megan stood up. "But we do have to give tender care to the dear body of the baby we loved."

For a second, looking at her, into her great, hurt blue eyes, Stowe's face softened. I would have kissed him, thought Carrie, pitying them both. Poor things.

"The church?" Stowe asked.

"I expect the Rector to come."

"But no friends . . ."

"We need friends, Stowe."

"Not me. I'm beyond that. All right. You face your friends, and the burial, and the Rector — me, I have to face the Law. Didn't you hear? I shot a man. That changes everything, Megan. It changes my life, and it will change yours. But you wanted all this . . ."

Megan began to weep again. Carrie led her back to the couch. "She can't take any more," she reminded Stowe. "Either find a way to help her bear this terrible grief, or let her alone."

"She grieves because she is remembering that I fought surgery on Bob. She can't face the fact that I was right."

Carrie bristled then. "You were not right!" she cried angrily. "Bob was much too ill to live without surgery. Suppose *you* face *that* fact!"

"Why don't you go home?" Stowe asked her, coldly, wearily. "Megan and I have things to decide. I have to leave, of course. The police will be here. But there are a few details . . ."

Again it was Megan who rose and went to him. "You can run," she agreed. "You can make any move you want, Stowe. You can leave, or I will. You are free."

He stood shaking his head. For the minute, Carrie was sorry for the man. "I won't be free, ever," he said grimly. Then he looked at his wife. "Nor will you be," he assured her. "Because, the same things that created our marriage now tie me to you. And you can see what it is like to be tied and held. The sash of a little boy's blue bathrobe will tie us together, Megan. And I don't think we are going to like that very much."

He spoke so forcefully that even Carrie could see that blue sash winding itself around those two.

This sounded like pure bathos, but it was not. Looking back, Carrie knew that it was only the terrible sad fact. At the time she had not understood fully, or clearly, but now she knew, and was horrified to know, that her sister and Stowe knew the truth and spoke the truth. Megan had schemed and planned to marry Stowe. She loved him, but that made little difference. Stowe knew that she loved him, and the way she had got him was the way she had kept him. He would not tolerate scandal, nor even snickering gossip. For him his marriage must appear, it must *be,* normal. Now, the death of their son must be encased in the proper ritual and ceremony.

Only — now he had a greater thing to escape. His terror, his panic, and his anger, too, that fate had stepped in to tear the smooth, conventional fabric of the marriage he had been maintaining . . . Oh, he had loved Bob! He most certainly had. The child had put meaning to his marriage; he was almost reconciled . . .

Why then must all be spoiled? He had asked a hundred times why the boy should become ill; he asked now why he had had to die. And there were few answers to those questions.

So he was frightened. So he had thought first of himself when he brought the gun to the hospital, when he had fired it and run —

Confusion heaped upon confusion. Stowe's mind and thoughts must be churning into a fearsome whirlpool. Leaving poor Megan with nothing, with nobody, to console her, to reassure her. Never had there been a case where so many things were right, and could appear to be wrong. Megan now was saying that she supposed she had done wrong to enforce surgery.

"We could have kept him for a while longer," she said.

"But you had the very best of advice," Carrie attempted to console her, because Stowe would not.

"Sure, sure," cried Stowe. "We gave him the best of everything. We put him into a hospital that just this year ranked among the top ten in the country. It has done that for several years. And credit is given to its fine medical school. It appoints all its chiefs of staff and selects only the best medical physicians and surgeons from that school. So almost any doctor could have killed my little boy this morning."

"Stop it!" Carrie cried in anguish. "Stop it, and get a hold on yourself! In time you will come to realize the truth of this whole matter. I am sorry Bob became ill. I am sorry, as sorry as I can be, for you and Megan. I am sorry for myself. Dear God, am I *sorry!* But —"

Stowe stood up. "I'll have to leave," he said, almost in his usual precisely courteous tone. "I think I should be running away from the police.

"Or should I just call the police, tell them where I am and give myself up? Megan! How are you going to like being Mrs. Murderer? Cold blood or premeditated, it makes no difference." He started for the stairs, turned and looked back at the two women. "I wonder how Tuck Fairbairn felt when he knew I was going to kill him? And tell me, Carrie, my darling, are all the prestigious doctors at your complex of so-called health and care as bad as the man you planned to marry?"

Carrie watched him disappear. She could not speak. How much shock could a person take? she wondered. How did one handle a person suddenly, or even progressively, gone insane?

Stowe was not rational, certainly. Would he be dangerous if she tried to detain him? Or tried to talk to him further? He had always been such a reserved, quiet man —

He came downstairs carrying a small bag. Carrie stepped before the outer door. "Stowe," she said firmly, "you simply cannot leave. I don't blame you for being . . ."

He dropped the bag, and put his hands on her shoulders. Yes, he was dangerous. Carrie stood quiet.

"I suppose," said Stowe, "that you think I should stay around. Open the front door when the bell rings, as we did when your parents died, Carrie. But they were not murdered! And I had not shot the man who let them die. Oh, no. Their deaths were natural, there was no question of violence. So the little ladies come in with their bowls of congealed salad, their offerings of pie and cake, their mumbled phrases of condolence. 'So sorry!' " His voice rose in a falsetto. " 'My condolences. It was all for the best, my dears . . .' "

Sadly, listening, Carrie remembered the parade of well-meaning friends. Today, while Stowe had been upstairs, Megan had spoken to just such a neighbor at the back door.

"But knowing you have friends will help, Stowe," she insisted. "As for the shooting, Tuck won't file charges. He . . ."

Stowe stared at her. "I did my damnedest," he said loudly. "Didn't the fellow die? Are you sure?"

"I am sure. Anyway, a dozen people could tell that you were out of your mind."

"I did kill him," Stowe said woodenly. "And you think the plea should be by reason of insanity. Let me go, Carrie. Get away from the door."

She moved away; he went out, and they heard his car start.

The "man" from the undertaking establishment did come, and the Rector. Carrie stayed with her, but Megan was able to talk to both of them. "She's in shock," said Megan's sister. "I'll bring the clothing to you. Don't ask her now . . ."

The Rector accepted the wish that there be no funeral or visitation. "Where is Mr. Vashon?" asked the clergyman.

Megan looked at him blankly. "I don't know," she said. "This whole thing has been difficult. We don't any of us realize . . ."

"Of course not. I'll be back later in the day."

"I think I am going to lie down," Megan told her sister when the good man had left.

"Fine," said Carrie, and helped Megan change to a robe, covered her with an afghan, shaded the bedroom, and went downstairs again. Sheer exhaustion would make her sister sleep perhaps.

But it was not very good for Carrie to be alone, either. She lighted the fire on the hearth. She made some toast and drank some tea. Catching sight of herself in the glass of a window, she combed her hair, and put on lipstick. Then she called the hospital, as she had been wanting to do for the past hour. She felt sure that she should warn Tuck that Stowe was still on the loose, and with that gun. Anyway, she wanted contact with him. If only for the reassurance of his strength, the sound of his firm and hearty voice.

But his secretary said that he had left the hospital.

"Where did he go?"

"He didn't say, Carrie. And I don't know. Nobody seems to know."

"How was he? When he left."

This worried her. Tuck would have had a busy day scheduled; he was not one to abandon his duties. So — where had he gone? She knew that for all his cloak of professional calm, he had taken Bob's death hard. He had grown fond of the child in the weeks out at the lake. He had given close, sorrowful attention to the child's illness. He had acknowledged the facts, but sorrowfully. He had expected to operate himself, to do a meticulous job of trying to remove all cancerous material, to save Bob years of life and accomplishment. Not that he was feeling that Don Moore had not done such a job. But Tuck had *wanted* to do it. He was the Chief Surgeon, there to help children like Bob.

The rash on his hands must have really confounded him. He had said enough — but what he was feeling inside would be hard even for Carrie to realize. If she could go to him, seek to comfort and reassure him . . . Where *was* he?

She must find him and talk to him.

She would get in her car and start right out. He probably had gone back to the lake, to his "cabin." If Carrie went there too, she might be able only to sit quietly and let her presence warm and soothe his hurt. She wanted to do this. But upstairs, under the soft woolen afghan, was Megan, Bob's mother, grieving, grieving. Stowe had gone berserk; he was of no comfort to his wife. So — Megan needed Carrie. She was in a really bad condition.

About the death of her child, of course.

And about Stowe. It wasn't that she loved him any more and wanted him with her. While Carrie had helped her undress, Megan had told her sister, solemnly, resignedly, that she felt she hated Stowe.

"Now," she had said, "he will convince himself that he was right, all along. He'll play the martyr, misunderstood and hurt by all of us. We made him lose Bob. We mistreated him, and prevented Stowe . . ."

Carrie had quieted her, and given her a sleeping pill. But — had there been some truth in what Megan had said? Was Stowe the martyr? The injured one?

Eight

Meanwhile . . .

Tucker Fairbairn attended to the paper work necessary for a death. He watched a nurse pack Bob's belongings into a carton, and asked an orderly to put them in the trunk of his car. He checked on the day's routine; he checked on Moore, who was profanely against being confined to bed. "You look a damn sight worse than I do," he assured the Chief.

"I started with a handicap. What can I get you? The morning paper, a cup of bouillon? Do you want a TV set?"

Moore graphically defined what he did not want. Why didn't Tuck get to work?

"I have dermatitis, doctor," said Tuck delicately.

"Still bad?"

"Not bad. But still there. I've been written off o.r.s and dressing rooms."

"So now what do you do?"

"Get out of these rompers and find Stowe Vashon."

"Do you think you should?"

"Midmorning today, I stopped thinking I knew what I should do, Donald."

"Aw, Tuck . . ."

"I'll change, and my hands won't look much better, so I am ready to admit that my nerves, which I thought I didn't have, are shot to hell."

"Have you ever had this reaction before?"

"Never. But I never had nerves before."

"You were too close to this case. What with Carrie, and all."

"Maybe so. It's a bit late to decide that. But I am not worrying about Carrie. It's Stowe I have to find."

"Where do you think he is?"

"I don't know. I don't know."

"Send me a bagel," Moore called after him. "And a can of beer."

"Sure," drawled Tuck. "Sure I will."

So Tuck changed from his hospital gear into the plaid cotton shirt, and the faded corduroy trousers which he had put on early that morning. Five hours ago? Yes, just about that. He picked up his shearling jacket and signed out at the desk.

"You could conduct classes, and see patients," Dr. Billings advised him.

"So I could," Tuck agreed amiably. And

he went straight to the elevator. Even before it reached the garage level, he was asking himself where he would go to look for Vashon. To the house in Edgewood, first, he supposed. The pretty light green and hand-hewn shingle house out in the upper-middle-class suburb.

There he found three cars. Carrie's, Megan's small one, and a strange black sedan. But not Stowe's white-top LTD, which had been pointed out to him one day during the time Stowe was coming to the hospital, parking his car, but avoiding Dr. Fairbairn like the plague. So — Vashon was not at home.

Had Tuck missed him at the hospital? Would he still be there? Scarcely. Not after shooting a doctor he had thought to be Tuck.

Of course he could have left town; it was more likely that he would have sought a friend, another lawyer, perhaps, for advice. But who were Stowe Vashon's friends? Tucker simply did not know the man, had not known him. Even after Carrie had come back into his life, he had seldom seen Megan; he never went to the Vashon home. Last summer with the girls up at the lake with Bob, perhaps Vashon had spent some time there. But not while Tuck was about.

And someone had said something about Stowe's not liking woods and the wild lake shore.

Normally he would now be with his wife in their grief, letting their friends come to them. But this certainly was not a normal circumstance. Stowe Vashon had shot a man. Not Tucker Fairbairn, who probably, who *certainly*, had been his target. He thought he had shot Tuck, he had seen the green-clad man crumple and slump to the floor. He must have thought he had killed Fairbairn, and had fled.

Of course, even as things were, the police still wanted him. Any gun shot required their attention. So — Tucker could ask about that. Did they know where Stowe Vashon was?

He was told that there was a pick-up order on him, Dr. Fairbairn, but since Dr. Moore was not badly hurt, they had not pressed his apprehension. He was a well-known attorney; he would turn himself in.

Under normal circumstances, yes, he would. But now, this noontime —

Tuck's last resort was Stowe's law office. He might be there. If he was not, his friends and associates, his secretary, would know his habits well enough to suggest places where he might be. They'd mention his home and give the address, but there might be other leads. Where did the man eat lunch, or go for a drink? Who was his barber? Crazy ideas like that crossed Tuck's mind as he drove into the city. Maybe Vashon would be at a library — even a movie. He could have picked up a bus — or a plane.

He need not run! All Tuck wanted to tell him was that he need not run.

The law firm of a half-dozen names was in one of the city's old, dignified, stone and brown marble buildings. The lobby extended from one street through to another. The high ceiling was arched, and painted with points of legal history. Justice — or Liberty? — with her scales and blindfold. The Dred Scott trial — others. There was a deal of old and ornate brass. Letter slots, directory frames, things like that — and a uniformed attendant in the elevator who said, "Good morning, sir," to the roughly dressed man with his tumbled black hair. Yes, sir! Mr. Vashon's office was on the fifth floor. It occupied the entire floor . . . "Here you are, sir!"

And there Tuck was, stepping out upon a parquetry floor, facing a middle-aged receptionist who let her horn-rimmed glasses drop from a chain to the bosom of her dark blue, tailored dress.

"Yes, sir?" she asked softly.

Tuck's eyes circled the room. Paneled doors opened from it. There were oil portraits on the paneled walls.

"I am Tucker Fairbairn," said the tall man in the shearling coat. "Doctor Fairbairn. And I am trying to find Mr. Stowe Vashon."

"Oh, sir," said the woman, "Mr. Vashon is not in the office today. There has been a death in his family. If you would state your business, perhaps one of the associates . . ."

"Could I speak to his secretary? Or does he have — in medicine we call them interns. I believe law clerk would be the term? Or maybe one of the partners. You see, it is very important that we locate Mr. Vashon."

"I understand, but — Oh, just a minute. Mr. Mayberry, sir?" She slurred the last two syllables of the name in an elegant fashion.

She said the name again to Tuck. "Mr. Mayberry is closely associated with Mr. Vashon. Both are corporation — Yes, Mr. Mayberry, if you have a moment. This gentleman is earnestly searching for Mr. Vashon, sir."

Mr. Mayberry was middle-aged, and clothed in the best-looking tweed suit Tuck had ever seen. "I gotta have one just like it!" he told himself.

"I hope you can help me," he said intently. "I am looking for Stowe Vashon because —"

Mr. Mayberry set down a rather beat-up box which he had been carrying. Covered with leather, rubbed and worn, the box had brass corners, and a brass plate on the end of it. Tuck leaned toward it curiously. Mr. Mayberry was explaining about Vashon's absence from the offices.

Tuck straightened. "Yes, sir. I know about his son's death. It was sudden, unexpected, and Mr. Vashon took it very hard. He blamed the surgeon on the case and I am afraid he resorted to violence."

Attorney and receptionist looked at each other in shocked surprise.

"The police did call . . ." said the woman.

"What . . . ?"

"They asked if Mr. Vashon was at the office, sir."

Mayberry turned to Tuck. "What sort of violence?" he asked quietly.

"I am afraid he shot the surgeon whom he held responsible for the child's death."

"Oh, no!"

"Yes, he did, sir. He has been in a somewhat hysterical state ever since he was told the boy had cancer . . ."

"Are you one of the doctors, sir?"

"I am *the* doctor. Fairbairn, orthopedic surgeon."

"Oh, yes. I recognize the name. Vashon . . ."

Tuck nodded. "I can imagine what he has said about me, and the terms he used."

"There was a court order. We took that hard in these offices, Dr. Fairbairn. We may keep our files in leather boxes, and we do. But we never before have had such a summons issued here."

"I have never before asked for one. But it was a matter of saving the boy's life."

"I understand that."

"Mr. Vashon did not."

"But if the boy died . . ."

"He suffered cardiac arrest before the surgery was well started, sir."

"And you say Vashon shot you?"

Evidently gunpowder had never been smelled in these offices, either.

"He didn't shoot me. Let me go back and explain —"

Tuck tried. He said that he wanted to find Vashon and tell him that Moore was not badly hurt, that no charges were being filed. That his wife needed him —

"But now he seems to have disappeared."

"He has?" asked Mr. Mayberry. "Why?

Why should he run — if he has."

"He thinks . . ."

"But he is a lawyer. I confess we are deeply shocked, Dr. Fairbairn." Then he suggested that they go to his own office. Where they would not be disturbed.

The office was not large. The walls were oak-paneled where they were not entirely covered by lawbooks, their leather bindings scruffy from long and hard use. There was an oriental rug on the gleaming wood floor, a handsome walnut desk, a high-backed leather chair, and a comfortable armchair where he invited Dr. Fairbairn to be seated. Would he like coffee?

Tuck was about to refuse, then agreed that he could take coffee. "I haven't eaten a thing since very early this morning," he admitted.

"But, sir —"

Again Tucker attempted to tell about Bob, and Vashon's opposition to surgery. "But I am a specialist, sir. The cancer was spreading. Amputation was our only recourse . . ."

Mr. Mayberry winced.

"It *is* a tragic thing," Tuck agreed. "But drastic measures are often our only, and in this case, the last resort. We could not persuade Mr. Vashon of that. He would not talk to me. His mother — the boy's mother — was more knowledgeable and finally she attained the court order."

"Did you expect the child to die?"

"It was major surgery, but no, we were not prepared for death. His heart simply stopped. I am sure you have seen television programs with the little sea-horse figure pinging its way across a green screen. This morning, it just stopped pinging. To us that meant the heart had died, a clot probably had shut off the artery — an autopsy will have shown us where and how."

"You did an autopsy on a *child?*"

"We do an autopsy on all deaths in our hospital, sir. It is a teaching hospital, and pathological examination is one of the ways . . ."

"That alone could have revolted Vashon."

"If he thought about it, I am sure it did. But, actually, I think the fact that he carried a gun and used it was what panicked him."

"And we must indeed locate him. He might do something foolish, doctor . . ."

"Yes, he might. We want to prevent that, to reassure him, and take him home to his wife, who needs him."

"Yes, I imagine she does. Well, let's see now. I know you have looked in the obvious places . . ."

"Yes. He is not at his home or the hospital."

"Nevertheless, I think I shall call his home."

"Certainly, sir."

But Stowe was not there. Yes, he had been, but he had left. "I'm afraid he was agitated, Mr. Mayberry."

So the gentleman in his superb tweed suit, his excellent haircut, his flawless white collar and exactly knotted dark tie faced the surgeon who looked like a backwoodsman with a shave.

"If he had cronies," said Tuck. "Or a favorite bar where he could sit and think. A library, perhaps — one of the people here in whom he might confide and from whom he could accept advice."

"Yes," said Mr. Mayberry, now showing his own rising concern. "I am somewhat at a loss," he confessed to Tuck. "This sort of impulsive behavior is not at all like the man. But you know that."

"I am afraid I do not, sir. He has avoided me from the time his son became ill. There are people who have phobias against what they call quack practitioners."

"I do myself when a dental appointment rolls around."

"So do I. But —"

"Are the police after him, Dr. Fairbairn?"

"Not as a criminal. But I am sure they want to talk to him. You just don't fire guns at doctors in a crowded surgical area without —"

"No, you do not. Even if you don't hit anybody."

"He did hit Dr. Moore, my assistant. He mistook him for me. That isn't hard to do in our rig of gown and cap and mask."

"You sound as if your position at the hospital is important, doctor."

"I am Chief of Orthopedic Surgery. My specialty is bone diseases."

"And you are well known, by all but me."

"I hope you never have to know me well, sir. In my field, I mean."

"I understand. So there was a gun shot, which alone brings in a police investigation."

"Yes, sir, it does. But no assault charges have been filed. Moore understands it was a matter of mistaken identity."

"He is your friend."

"He is my assistant, and just as capable a surgeon as you would ever find. But, yes, I think he is my friend. When, this morning, my hands developed this rash —" He spread his hands on the desk top. The rash was disappearing rapidly.

"Of course. You could not operate. Now! Just what is it you want of me? To help you find Vashon?"

"I had hoped he might be here in the office."

"The receptionist would know if he were. Now, let's see. I called his home. I was told he had been there, but had left."

"I know that is what happened. But if you could give me some personal leads — maybe even the name of a lady friend."

"Or a bartender . . ."

"Yes, sir. In some cases, those would be refuges for a man in his state."

"You think he is disturbed?"

For a minute, Tuck sat thoughtful. "Yes, sir," he said then. "Even in a medical sense, I do think the man is disturbed. Certainly irrational. He already has acted impulsively, under the pressure of grief or even terror. I'd be disturbed, wouldn't you?"

"Given time to imagine myself — However, Stowe Vashon has always seemed to be a most self-controlled man. But if at present he is not, I can understand your wanting to know where he is, possibly to protect the other man, the one he thinks is you."

"Oh, surely that mistake has been pointed out to him."

"Then you would need to protect yourself, wouldn't you?"

The police, agreeing to give Tuck time to find Vashon, had brought up that point.

"Or others on the surgical staff."

Tuck shook his head, and brushed his dark hair back from his face. "No," he said, "what I would like is to see him reconciled with his wife. They have been bitterly at odds over the need for surgery. But the boy's death — they both dearly loved the child. He was certainly an appealing youngster, bright —" The doctor's shoulders shook. "I myself am struck with the tragedy of his death. I can only imagine what it must mean to his mother and to his father. But if they could face that tragedy together, realize its horror, look each to the other for comfort, or at least rationalization —"

"Do you think that would be possible?"

"Not at once. Not immediately. But if they could be brought together, and in some way would give themselves the time to work through their present emotions — then they might not lose all they could have . . ."

"You look far ahead, don't you, Dr. Fairbairn?"

"My profession deals with life. Not with an immediate problem, such as the amputation of a child's leg, but with the life that amputation might afford the little boy who could grow into a fine man, a productive man."

"I see. I don't think I have known any doctors like you."

"I am sure you have. And lawyers, too."

"Would you like me to go with you when you hunt for Stowe?"

"Oh, no," Tuck decided. "I believe we'd do better if this particular disaster were not closely connected with his law practice. He will need an anchor of some sort."

"You don't think his wife . . . ?"

"Megan is a fine person."

"I know her, of course. Not well. She is good-looking. Why did she marry Vashon?"

Tuck looked surprised. "She fell in love with him. I suppose that explains most marriages."

"I hope you are right. Now, for places where Vashon might be."

He drew paper toward him, and listed names. Stowe liked to walk along the lake esplanade sometimes, he said. He often read in the main public library, only three blocks from the office. There was an old courthouse where the scene of a famous trial had been held, and which was maintained. As for bars . . . He was not a heavy-drinking man, but there were grills, and, yes, bars . . .

"Why don't you want me to go along?" the attorney asked as he handed Tuck the list.

"Well, there are personal things, many of them. I have a deal of straightening out to do."

"I see."

He did not, of course. Tuck was thinking of that kiss in the dimly lighted hospital corridor. Carrie. And Stowe Vashon . . .

He stood up, and tugged down his jacket. "You can do one thing for me," he said.

"What is that?" asked the other man.

"Tell me who your tailor is."

"But why? Your clothes suit you. I couldn't get away with them."

Slender, well-proportioned limbs, smooth, well-cut hair, smooth, regular-featured face — no, he could not wear Tuck's rough clothes.

"I am going to marry a girl," said the doctor, "who thinks I can look better than I do."

"Will she marry you, anyway?"

"Oh, yes, I think so. But I would like to see her eyes if I should produce the effect you do."

The attorney laughed. He took a card from his billfold and wrote a name on it. "I am glad Vashon didn't shoot you," he said, handing it across to Tuck.

"He is going to be glad too," said Dr. Fairbairn. "Shall I tell you how things work out?"

"I think I'll know," said his new friend. "And if I ever need medical advice —"

"Don't need my kind, please," said Tuck earnestly. "But, yes, call me. And — thank you very much."

"You haven't found Stowe yet."

"I shall. I shall."

He did find him, though it took some time. He went to the public library, he went to the Esplanade, and walked a mile one way, a mile back. He went to a hotel bar, and then he went to a bar called the Bismarck. It was an oyster bar, dimly lighted, where he found Stowe standing at the rail, watching a huge black man shuck oysters. Tuck stepped up beside him. "Are they good oysters?" he asked.

"Best available here in the middle of the country," said the black man.

"I didn't ask you," said Tuck. He turned, waiting for Stowe to answer. If the man recognized him . . .

He did not, though he did glance at Tuck. The rough clothes does it, the doctor decided.

"They're good," said Stowe. "I've already eaten a dozen."

"Fair enough," said Tuck, and nodded to the shucker.

"Beer, sir?"

Stowe was drinking beer.

Tuck nodded. "Beer," he agreed. "But not that light stuff."

"We don't serve it, sir."

"Good."

So the two men, one unknown to the other, yet so intimately connected, drank beer and ate oysters, comparing the dips. After twenty minutes or so, they moved to a booth and ordered oyster stew. It came, rich, thick, served with crackers, crusty bread, and sweet butter. And the two men talked, the tail, rough-haired man, the slender man, about his own age, with smooth red-blond hair and troubled green eyes.

Stowe told that he was a lawyer, and he was trying to decide if he might not have a malpractice suit over the death of a member of his family.

"There are an awful lot of them going on," said Tuck mildly. "Malpractice suits."

"There are. And probably with cause."

"Possibly, though I have heard that the contingent fees the lawyers are paid account for the number."

"I know that is claimed."

"It must be hard for people with small claims to get a lawyer to serve them. And wouldn't some lawyers make a good living building up big suits, getting their cuts of big awards?"

Vashon nodded. "They do that, of course. I am not in the racket myself. Just now I am interested in the possibility that such suits would insure better medical and hospital care."

"How would you insure that? Or even know it if you saw it? I have heard of imagined injuries that are hard to prove or disprove."

"Oh, yes. But I do think doctors should constantly have to take additional training, and be relicensed at frequent intervals."

"And lawyers too?" Tucker could feel the strangeness of this discussion with this particular man.

But they talked about it for some time. There should be some sort of federal commission. They mentioned doctors' strikes.

And their discussion might have been one between friends. It was strange.

It was very strange.

And then, as he buttered his second slice of french bread, Stowe talked about the death of his son. He spoke as a man remembering and recounting something long past. "They said it was bone cancer the boy had. But why should he have such a thing? A healthy little boy, racing and jumping. Yelling. I remember how often I had to tell him to quiet down. Do you know anything about such matters?"

"I have studied them to a degree," said Tuck slowly. He was tempted to identify himself, yet felt sure that Stowe, once he knew, would no longer talk calmly to him.

"I am sure there has never been a significant breakthrough as to the cause of cancer," he said thoughtfully. "I believe we would see headlines in the papers."

"But there must be *some* reason. Bob must have bruised his leg somehow . . ."

"He could have. Though I have read of many reasons being suggested as causes. Some say people are born with cells that can become cancerous. I even read of one case where glue sniffing — you know, the airplane glue the kids use on models. They get a high out of sniffing it. This article was sure it had caused cancer and death."

Stowe laid down his slice of bread. "I don't know why I am eating so much," he said. "I was hungry. I have been worried about the boy. I didn't want his leg cut off. I didn't want him —" He paused. "To die," he added softly.

"Of course you didn't. What about the child's mother? Maybe you should go home. Your wife probably needs you."

Stowe stood up. Suddenly his face was contorted with rage. "I should never have married that woman," he cried. "Then there would have been no Bob!"

"Your other children by another woman could have died of the same cause," said Tuck.

"But I should never have married Megan. I was in love with her sister, and Megan took me away from her!"

Shock and bitter anger rose in Tuck's throat. All these years Stowe Vashon had cherished that grudge. Tuck wanted to clench his fist, and strike out at this man, but even as he doubled his fingers into the palm of his hand, he saw the blisters rise.

"Did," he asked breathlessly, "did the sister love you?"

Vashon turned, "No," he said angrily. "No, she didn't. But what difference would that make? I loved her. I could have found a way. There are 'ways' with all women!"

It struck like a blow. Vashon did not know who Tuck was. How should he, his rough jacket, his corduroy trousers, his hair

. . . And not suspecting to whom he talked, he would speak the truth.

"Tell me this, Buster," Tuck said roughly, "are you down here mourning your son you say you loved, or are you trying to hurt your wife? For something she could not help either."

Without answering, Stowe put some money on the counter, and the two men walked out into the winter sunshine. It was early afternoon. This was proving to be a long, long day.

"My wife hurt me," then said Stowe, stubbornly. "She married me — she made me think I had to marry her. And I didn't. Well, never mind . . ."

"But you did have a son. There must have been some love."

"Agggh!" cried Stowe. "A man's a man. We were married. We bought a house, and there was this master bedroom. You sleep together in what is called a queen-sized bed. A man's a man — you don't need love, really."

"That must have been hard on the kid."

"No, it wasn't. I was good to him; we both were. I'll give Megan that. And the boy loved us both. We both loved him."

"But if the parents don't love each other — that still must have been hard on him.

Kids are smart these days."

"Yes, they are. Bob was. But then he began to limp. I blamed Megan for that."

"Why?"

"She was with him all day. She must have let him get hurt. He limped. She took him to the doctor. Then to another doctor who said he must have surgery. I objected. But the damn woman got a court order — and the doctor let him die. I knew he would, so I brought a gun to the hospital and I shot him."

"But, good Lord, man, you can't go around shooting *doctors!* Why, I could call that officer over there on the corner, and tell him who you are, what you've done . . ."

"What do you care?"

"I do care. Because even you might need that doctor some day. Besides, as a lawyer, you *know* why you can't go around shooting people."

"How do you know I'm a lawyer?"

"I know."

They stood there on the corner of the busy street. At the very far end of it, the lake waters sparkled and danced. Cars passed before them in a steady stream, horns blared, people talked and laughed. Slowly Tuck spread out his hands; they were covered with blisters. "There was another time, another place, where I couldn't operate . . ." he said slowly, almost absentmindedly. "Just as this morning I couldn't operate on your son."

Stowe stared at him. His eyes flaring, his mouth fallen open. "Are you telling me," he stammered, "that you are . . ."

"Tucker Fairbairn, yes. But it wasn't the surgery done that killed Bob. There was a blood clot . . ."

Stowe Vashon's hand caught at his shoulder. Tuck stepped back.

"You can't be Tucker Fairbairn," Stowe shouted hoarsely. "I killed you two — three hours ago. The police are hunting me . . ."

"The police are not 'hunting' you. They know where to find you. You didn't kill anybody."

"I tried," cried Stowe. "I sure as hell tried."

"Yes. You fired your gun, but you're a lousy shot. And you were aiming at the wrong man."

"He was the doctor. He came out of the operating room, all wrapped up in green clothes. He —"

"He was the doctor who began the surgery, yes. I developed this rash and could not operate. You shot —"

"You — you —"

"Moore is just as good a doctor as I am. There was no fault in the surgery done. The boy's heart just stopped beating. It happened without warning. Suddenly there was no pulse."

Stowe stared at him. Then he turned away, leaned against an ornate lamppost, greened with weather, and he beat his fists against it. Then he held his head in his hands. Tucker moved to shield his torment from the curious eyes of the passers-by. Certainly he would have chosen another place for this confrontation.

He put a strong hand on Vashon's shoulder. "Let's go somewhere," he said, "and talk a little about Bob."

Stowe turned to look at him, as he might have looked at someone he had never seen before. His eyes were red-rimmed. "It was no good at all, was it?" he asked. "There never was a chance . . ."

"We gave him what chance he had. But, no, it was no good.

"And I — I would do the same thing another time."

"Would you, really?"

With Tuck's hand still on his shoulder, Stowe began to walk slowly along the street.

A child ran past and ahead of them, and

the red-haired man looked at him curiously. "There is no use discussing it," he said dispiritedly. "I'll never have another chance, or another choice."

"Oh, yes, you will. I don't mean about what you'd do about another sick child, or about punishing a doctor who certainly did not need a bullet through his arm."

"You're right? I didn't kill him?"

"You didn't come close. He'll have a sore arm for a time. The police take a dim view of guns in hospitals. But — speaking of choices — we all have them, all the time. Shall we choose to step down this curb and cross the street? Or go around the corner? So what is your choice? To go home. Or to the police. Make a scene and sacrifice your career. Your surrender as a would-be murderer won't help your law business."

"But you said . . ."

"That they know about the shooting. But you know these things can be kept out of the papers. Moore isn't going to file charges."

"And you won't."

"What did you do to me? Beyond making me pop out in blisters."

"You mean all this, Fairbairn? You really mean it?"

"Of course I mean it."

"Then I guess I had better go home. Megan probably needs me."

"I suspect she does. Where is your car?"

"In a garage near the office. I — I was going to ask legal advice." He almost grinned. And Tucker did laugh.

"I'll tell Megan how I have felt about Carrie . . ."

"She knows. But maybe you should tell her. It will hurt, just as it hurts me, if only to wonder about Carrie's side of the matter."

They went to the garage, and Tuck drove Stowe's car home. His own probably would be towed off the street where he had left it. Unless he could taxi right back . . .

The trim green house stood serenely in the sunlight. Something should mark its tragedy, thought Tuck. The old way of a wreath at the door, or draped crepe . . .

Without speaking again to Tuck, Stowe went into the house. Tucker sat for a minute, shaking his head. There was a strange man. What would he find to say to Megan? What would she say to him?

And Carrie? He got out of the car, took the keys, went into the house and phoned for a cab without anyone's noticing him. He could hear Stowe talking to Megan upstairs. Carrie was nowhere about.

* * *

Megan met Stowe at the head of the stairs. She looked beyond him as if expecting to see someone with him.

She had changed her dress, and combed her hair. "You look terrible," Stowe told her.

"So do you. Where have you been?"

She went into the bedroom and he followed her. "I've been trying to get things straight in my head," he told her.

She glanced over her shoulder. "Did you manage it?" she asked. "Why don't you shower and change your clothes? People keep coming in."

"I don't want to talk to people. I want to talk to you."

"To me?" She sounded astonished.

"Yes. We have all sorts of things to say to each other."

"What about, Stowe?" she asked. "I did what I thought was best for Bob."

"And it wasn't enough. I know now that nothing would have been enough."

Outside, a horn sounded, and Megan stepped to the window, looked down. "It's a cab," she said in surprise.

"I suppose Fairbairn called one. He must have left his car downtown."

"But —"

"I could have driven him back for it. You could have. Just now, it seemed more important for me to talk to you. Where's Carrie?"

"She had some errand. She will be back."

Stowe sat down on the edge of the bed. "I have been with Fairbairn for the past two hours," he said.

"Drinking."

"I drank. He didn't. Oh, maybe, a beer."

She regarded her husband curiously. "Did he hunt for you?" she asked.

"Yes, he did. I think he wanted to keep my crazy behavior out of the papers."

"Can he?"

"He will try."

"You were in a frenzy. Bob —"

"I told him I had had an affair with Carrie."

"Did he believe you?"

"Don't you?"

"I believe you may have told him that, but I don't think he believed you."

"Why not, Megan?"

"Well, for one thing he knows, too, that you have been drinking."

"He didn't mention it."

"He didn't need to. He knows about the frenzy you've been in for the past week. And now . . ."

"You know? He's a man a fellow can talk to."

"Yes, he is. And if you had given him the chance, he could have smoothed things out for you about Bob."

"It wouldn't have changed one thing."

"Yes, it would, Stowe. It did for me. I was frantic to think we could lose our child. Tuck helped me accept what could not be changed. He might have done the same for you."

"I don't like doctors."

"You don't need to *like* them. But they know their job. Do all your clients like you?"

For a long minute, Stowe was silent. Then he lay back on the bed, and folded one arm over his eyes. "I am so tired," he said.

"Yes. But don't worry yourself over what you said to Tuck about Carrie."

"I said we'd had an affair."

"That doesn't matter. Not even if it's true. She's going to marry Tuck. She loves him."

"What did Tuck do to you," asked Carrie's voice from the hall, "when you told him about our great affair? Did he knock you down?"

Neither Megan or Stowe had heard her come into the house. How long had she listened?

She was carrying an armful of Bob's things, the folded blue robe, the puppets, an assortment of pajamas and books. She went across the hall to his room and put the things carefully away. She hung the robe on a hanger and put it in the closet. Stowe and Megan watched her.

"Don't cry, Carrie," Megan told her.

"It helps. Why don't you try it?" Carrie sounded angry. "And why don't you answer my question Stowe? Did Tuck knock you down?"

"No," said Megan's husband.

"Then he didn't believe you."

"He did, enough to break out in a rash."

The woman stared at him. It was Carrie who laughed. "I wondered about that," she said. "It has never happened to Tuck before."

Megan was getting out clean clothes for Stowe to put on, a gray suit, a white shirt, and a dark green tie. Underwear, socks.

He watched her. "Will you give me my bath too?" he asked, much in his old familiar, bitter tone.

"I could and would," she said. "But people will be coming to the house. From the office. Your friends — we've kept up appearances so far —"

He nodded. "Yes, we have. Carrie, will you excuse me?"

She flipped her hand. "Don't mind me," she said. There's that affair, remember. Besides, I'm a nurse, and men —"

"Carrie!" said Megan warningly.

"I'm going, I'm going!" she cried. "I'll even go down and fix us something to eat."

"But not . . ."

"No, sir. Nothing to drink. Because I understand even coffee is no help."

She disappeared, and Megan followed her. "He will be all right," she told her sister.

"Sure he will. As right as he'll ever get. If he were mine, I'd boot him out."

"Not if you loved him."

Carrie turned to look at Megan. Then she nodded. "I guess he does need you now," she agreed.

There were interruptions. People telephoned, a neighbor brought in part of a ham; flowers were delivered. Megan talked to the friends who came.

But by the time Stowe came downstairs, white-faced but quiet, only the family was there. He sat down at the kitchen counter and drank some milk. "I'm not hungry," he said. "I ate oysters . . ."

"Did Tuck?"

"I don't remember. He found me — and

waited until I would let him talk to me."

Megan sat beside him. "Stowe," she asked, after a time, "do you remember how and why you married me and not Carrie?"

Carrie made a small sound of protest.

"You don't need to listen," Megan told her.

"I seem to be in on this."

"Well, in a way." She turned back to Stowe.

"Was there a why?" he asked.

"Yes, there was. And you should remember. You took me to Chicago for a weekend . . ."

"And you forgot your house slippers."

Her eyes widened. "I'd forgotten that!" she said.

"Well, you did. But you had pretty feet."

"For heaven's sake," said Carrie. "Here we are . . ."

"We can't talk about Bob," said Megan firmly.

Carrie took her plate to the sink. "No," she agreed, "we can't. So we talk about things like your pretty feet. You do have pretty ones. High-arched. You can wear pretty slippers where I can't. I am more the flat-heeled, hiking type."

"You thought you were pregnant," Stowe told Megan, ignoring Carrie.

"I didn't get pregnant for five years," she said indignantly. "It was you who thought . . ."

"But you didn't get pregnant, did you?"

"Not for five years."

Carrie watched them, listening to them in amazement. She might as well not have been there.

"But I planned to marry you," Megan was saying. "And I did."

"Yes, you did."

"A lot of our friends thought it was because I had got you pregnant," Stowe added. "Did you know different then?"

"Of course I did."

"Then why in the devil . . . ?"

"I — because I loved you."

"Why can't you love me now, and let things rest at that?"

"Because now I know you are in love with Carrie."

"Look," Carrie interposed, "why are you talking about these things now?"

"We are talking about *Bob*," said Megan, turning to gaze at her solemnly.

Carrie stared at her. Yes, she supposed they were. And — "I think I'll go back to the hospital," she said, "and find Tuck."

Megan and Stowe paid no attention to her. She had never seen them so absorbed in each other. Polite, yes. Indifferent, often. But — at this time —

"I did love Carrie then," Stowe was saying. "I was counting on my fingers how long it would take for me to think she was old enough for me to ask her to marry me. She was just a kid, of course. Exquisite, and innocent."

Carrie fetched her coat from the hall closet. This day was incredible. These things simply were not happening.

"She was a sweet kid," Stowe was saying, as she went out the door. "A lot of men dream of marrying just such a girl."

"I suppose I was young and innocent myself once," Megan mused.

"You always were a nice person," her husband said earnestly. "But you had savvy. You —"

"Don't tell me what I was," Megan cried. "I know what I was. I was twenty-four years old, and I decided, at that age, I had to go after a man and get him."

Stowe drank a little milk. "I guess it was all right. And — I didn't have any affair with Carrie."

"Well, I know *that!*"

"I guess I knew all along that there never would be an affair. She doesn't even like me."

"She would if things had been different between you and me."

"But they never were any good, were they?"

"They could have been. They weren't too bad after Bob was born. And if he had lived . . ."

Stowe got up from the stool and walked to the back door. She thought he meant to leave. "We should have waited," he said. "But we weren't given that chance, were we? Now all we have left is this tragedy."

"Yes," said Megan. "It is tragedy." She began to weep. "We couldn't help his getting sick, but we could have — Well, now he is dead. And we can't ever be happy again. He used to like it when we did things together. He knew we were quarreling. He knew you hated his sore leg —"

"I hated its happening to him. And I am sorry — I truly am, Megan, that I fought you about trying to help him. Do you suppose . . . ?"

"Carrie told me that nothing would have saved him. There was the cancer, and the ruptured blood vessel —"

"But, before that, if we had made the decision together. If we could have — even if we were wrong — if we could say now that we did the best we could for him . . ."

"I know. I was wrong to go to court."

"You didn't go. Tucker Fairbairn did that."

"I let him. And I can understand that you cannot forgive me for doing it. Or him."

Stowe took a step toward her. He put one hand on her shoulder. "Megan," he said hoarsely, "about the hardest thing I ever do in my life is to say that I have been wrong. But I must say it now. You and Fairbairn probably were not wrong about Bob. And I was."

She stared at him. Her great blue eyes shaded by her thick lashes. Carrie's eyes. Bob's eyes. She put her fingertips to her lips. "But you hated us . . ."

"Yes, I did. I hated both of you, and feared you. Because you were *not* wrong. You two were so much braver than I could ever be. I watched you especially. Tucker is a doctor, and it's his business to know what is right in these cases. But you — I watched you. I would see you with Bob. I knew that you loved him. I knew that you could not bear any more than I could the need to cut off his leg. And yet, you knew it had to be done. And then I began to realize how much braver you were than I was. A man likes to think — But he's crazy! Often, *often* only a woman can know the blind love that is possible to motherhood. I recognized that. I wanted to feel it in myself. But I could not. I simply could not. It was beyond me. It was something, well, almost godlike.

"I couldn't feel it, or act upon it. But you, a mother, could. And God can. You know, suffer little children, the sparrow falls . . . There it was in you. If you could care that *much!* I couldn't, and the truth of that terrified me. I was so terrified that I thought it was something I could fight with a gun . . ."

Megan was weeping uncontrollably. "Oh, Stowe," she cried, "if I had guessed your suffering . . ."

He drew her to him, and held her against his shoulder; he smoothed her soft, dark hair. "How could you know what I could not see for myself?" he asked. "How could you?"

The doorbell rang, and the telephone. They did not heed their clamor. Stowe wiped the tears from her face, he kissed her. They need talk no more for a time.

"Do you know what we are doing?" Stowe asked, stroking her arm. "We are making love, Megan. You and I. For the first time . . ."

She looked up at him. "I've told you many times that I loved you."

"Yes, I know. And I have said nothing."

"Oh, yes. You told me that you hated me."

"Isn't there something about love and hate . . . ?"

She nodded. "I hope so. I hope so." Then she sighed. "If Bob could see us as we are now, he would be so pleased."

Stowe said nothing. He moved away from her, and began to clear the dishes from the counter. "Maybe — do you think maybe he lived for this?" he asked gravely.

She began to weep again. "It was too great a price. He thought — I thought — that you hated me."

"I told him that I did."

"Oh, Stowe, you didn't."

"I am afraid I did. I said you wanted him — Tuck, or somebody, had told him that he was going to be crippled. He said he didn't mind too much. That he could be a lawyer, or a doctor, or even sail a ship with only one leg. And then, when I said that I hated the whole thing, he told me that I couldn't hate you. Because mothers were not to be hated. And that's when I knew what an awful thing I was doing, to fight you, to keep away from you. Bob was being brave, and you were. I guess I know now that Tuck was being brave too."

"Yes, he was. He loved Bob."

"He — where is he now? Where did he go?"

"He left. For the hospital, I suppose."

"He hunted for me this morning, and talked to me."

"He knew how hurt you were."

"He knew how crazy-angry I was. And yet, do you know what he asked me, Megan? He asked me what I would do another time. If I had another child, he meant."

She turned to look at him. She took a step toward him. "What would you do?" she asked.

"I don't know. I talk about learning a lesson, and mother love, and all that. I probably never will find out, of course, if I meant all I said about mother-love, and stuff."

She reached him, and looked up into his face. "Yes, you will know, Stowe," she said softly. "That's why Tuck asked you. He knows that I am pregnant, that there is another child on the way."

He stared at her. He slapped his hands together, and turned away from her. He was in complete panic. "Not another *baby!*" he shouted at her.

She smiled at him.

"But when?" he asked. "How?"

286

"Do you remember when you sent me and Bob up to the cabin on the lake? Bob was limping, and you said I was looking awful. That was your word. Awful."

"I thought you were worrying about Bob."

"I was. But —"

"But what will you do, Megan? You can't go through all this again! You couldn't."

"I wouldn't give up Bob's four years of life, would you? And Tuck says there is no reason to think that this child will have cancer."

"Oh, what does he know!"

"He knows. And even if such a thing should happen, Tuck probably could save this one. He saves children like Bob all the time. And it wasn't the cancer that killed Bob. He had an aneurysm, a clot, in his abdomen. They did an autopsy, and Carrie said —"

"An autopsy on *Bob?*" Stowe was horrified.

"Of course. They do autopsies on all such patients. In order to learn, and to help the next child."

"Our next child," said Stowe, savoring the words.

"Yes. Our next child," she repeated. "And Tuck will take care of it."

Stowe nodded his head up and down. "Yes, I believe he will," he said. "He knows I am a rat."

"You're not."

"Yes, I was."

"Then I was too. To marry you when I knew you didn't love me."

"Things change, Megan," he said softly. "Maybe we will change. Maybe we can relax and enjoy this child. And share him all the way."

"And love him, all the way. If Bob has taught us that — if we can learn —"

"We are talking like a couple of maudlin fools," he said crossly, "but maybe even fools can learn about love."

"I think we have learned all we need to learn about that," said Megan sensibly. "So I'll clear away the dishes, and you answer that crazy telephone."

Tuck left the Vashon house, wondering what he was leaving behind. Could Stowe be trusted? What had become of that gun? How safe would Megan be? And Carrie? When he got his own car, he thought he should drive back there, but he went to the hospital instead. He looked at it with new eyes, as if he had never seen it before, as if he had never driven down into the garage, nor walked the halls so familiar to him. He only nodded when people spoke to him, and was aware that they turned to watch him.

Well, he was grieving about Bob. The boy's death was a throbbing hurt in his chest. What could he have done differently? Could he have saved him? Why hadn't he pursued the matter of that aneurysm, that clot? He had guessed one was there. He would still have had to operate, but . . .

Upstairs he changed to a white lab coat over greens, and asked to have his schedule and the Vashon autopsy report sent to his office.

"Are you all right, doctor?" asked Mrs. Adams.

"Yes, I'm all right. Not good. Is there any schedule left? How about Dr. Moore?"

"He's fine. We had to sedate him to keep him in bed."

"I'll look in on him."

Mrs. Adams herself brought the report sheet, and the schedule. "We are all so sorry . . ." she attempted.

Tuck glanced up at her. "Let's not talk too much about that," he suggested. "We did what we had to do. Now — Oh, lordy, what is this consultation about?"

"The Sly baby was born this morning, sir."

Tuck stared at her. "The Sly baby?" he asked.

"Yes, sir. We had orders — Maternity had orders —"

Tuck gasped. "I remember. Two babies — both died — adrenal — Where is your consultation, Adams?"

"They took the baby immediately to Children's."

"And you couldn't find me."

"No, sir, we couldn't. But the pediatricians and the O.B. man thought they knew —"

Tuck was on his feet and going out of the office. That baby . . . Mrs. Sly had lost two children in infancy. When she had shown up at Maternity, again pregnant, her case had been made the focal point of the doctors who were trying to detect birth defects in time to prevent . . . This child might have no defect, but at least ten M.D.'s were going to see if it did."

"Send Tennant if you can find him," he called back to the Floor Head. "If Moore weren't goofing off . . . Imagine, being asleep at three in the afternoon!"

It was good to have Dr. Fairbairn striding through the halls, talking to himself or to anyone he met. It was good to have him come into the consultation room, and be allowed to say, "Hi!" to the other medics. "What do we have?"

The other Sly babies had had adrenal deficiencies. Which might have been treated if detected, and the babies saved. This child, a husky boy, was now busily sucking three fingers of his hand.

"Looks like he could get behind a plow tomorrow," said Tuck, patting the little fellow, reaching his other hand for the chart.

"Nothing?" he asked when he had read it.

"Heart, lungs, blood — we can't find a thing, Tuck."

But he himself must undress the infant and feel its bones, test its reflexes, move each joint. "Nothing," he said thankfully. "Does the mother know?"

"That we can't find anything. Especially that the adrenal situation —"

"Well, thank the Lord for that!" said Tuck fervently. "But keep an eye out," he told the pediatrician, "and for at least six weeks. I've got to run. I'm six hours behind myself."

They knew he was, and why he was. They would talk about Bob in staff meetings. For now . . .

For now he wanted to find Carrie. He called the Vashon house and got no answer.

He called her apartment. Now he must wait until she got in touch with him. But he had to see her. He *had* to! After what Stowe had told him, the man was not to be believed under the circumstances. Half-drunk, crazed with his anger and grief, frightened by his shooting the doctor he thought he had shot . . .

Tuck didn't believe Vashon, and even if he did it wouldn't make any difference, but he had to see Carrie. To look into her eyes, and find trust there. To touch her hand, to —

He must conceal this impatience. He must go over and speak to Mrs. Sly; he must talk to people, and listen to some fellow — the Chaplain, Lord love him! who thought he could comfort Dr. Fairbairn. He had heard about the rash . . .

"Moore was doing a very fine job," Tuck told him gruffly.

"I hope you persuaded him of that," said Mr. Swift.

"I am boss. He will believe me."

"I expect he will. What caused the rash, Tuck?"

"If I knew, I'd tell you, Padre. But I don't know. Strange things happen to strange people."

"They really do." The Chaplain was going through the tunnel step for step for Tuck, who wanted to run. Maybe he could have Carrie paged. "And we never know where we will find the strangest of them all. I remember my first pastorate. I was only a curate, of course. We work up in the church the way you chaps do in medicine. But this was a fine, big church, with lots of rich people. But even among all those rich ones, there was one chap who stood out. He wore — not always, but often — he wore the most beautiful cream-colored suede suit. It was really exquisite. But do you know, after service, every Sunday, he would go to the parish hall, where about half the congregation went. He would pour himself a cup of coffee, add cream and sugar, and then that meticulous man would take off his glasses and stir the stuff with one of the ear pieces."

Tuck looked at him. "Why did you tell me that?" he asked.

The Reverend Mr. Swift smiled. "To divert your thoughts," he said. "You are not a man who needs consolation or preaching."

Tuck pressed an elevator button. "I am glad someone knows the kind of man I am," he said gently. "By the way, sir, if you should see Carrie Reynolds, tell her that I am hunting her."

"Oh, I'll do that, Tuck. And I'll tell her about the Sly baby too."

"You do that. One of your messages should please her." He stepped into the elevator. This just had to be the strangest day of his whole life!

Oyster bars, and a little boy's blue bathrobe. The healthy Sly baby, and — He looked down at his hands. There was only a small blister or two.

. . . and the new baby coming into the Vashon family. Should Megan abort that child? How would Vashon behave? He had loved Bob, there was no question about that. But another child to love, and perhaps lose? Or to raise, always fearful of losing it? Should Tuck suggest psychiatry, counseling of some kind for both Megan and Stowe?

And for Tucker Fairbairn? Did Carrie know she had promised to marry a nervous Nellie? One who would break out in blisters?

What *had* she thought that morning? Pity? Embarrassment? Maybe even relief that the decision had been taken from Tuck. Some day he would ask her . . .

He strode through the halls, passed along the tunnels that connected the buildings. He met almost everybody. He was sure that he did.

"What's the joke of the day, Tuck?" some would ask as they passed.

He didn't reply to the first of these. Then: "It's getting near that time of year when all the party bores will want to bet you that you can't name all eight of Santa's reindeers."

"Can you?" one nurse asked him unexpectedly.

And he laughed. To his own surprise. "I'll bone up," he called after the young woman.

Having reached Skull and Bones, he decided that he was ready to look in on Moore.

He found that doctor sitting up in bed, being entertained by his wife.

"He can read for himself," Tuck told Sarah Moore.

"I so seldom get him where he can't go off on a call," she told Tuck.

Tuck picked up the chart. He pursed his lips. "Move over," he said to the man in the bed. "I must feel worse than you do."

"How're your hands?" asked Dr. Moore.

Tuck held them out.

"Body?"

"If you think I'm going to do a striptease with only Sarah for an audience . . ."

Dr. Moore grinned. "You'll be able to work tomorrow."

"Well, I thought so too. I just came in to see if I could see through the hole in your arm."

So he was laughing when he went into the hall, and almost knocked Carrie down.

"Where in thunder have you been?" he asked her, surprised.

"*Tuck!* Where have *you* been?" she asked him. She reached for his hand, and then the other. "They're doing all right, aren't they?" she asked.

"I offered to show Sarah Moore my tummy, but you know these jealous husbands."

He opened his office door and pushed her inside. "Adams!" he called before closing the door.

She looked up from the floor desk, and nodded.

"Now," said Carrie, sitting down in his chair. "Where . . . ?"

"I forget where I saw you last. I hunted for Stowe, and I took him home."

"I knew you were hunting him, but I thought you had taken him to jail."

She was in uniform, and Tuck stood looking down at her. The Sly baby is healthy," he told her.

"Oh, good. How — Maybe you did take Stowe to jail when you took him home. I mean, in a manner of speaking. What do you suppose Megan is going to *do?*"

"Bob did more to bring those two together than he did to separate them."

Carrie thought about this. "Would you like your chair, doctor?" she asked politely.

"Megan has told him about the new baby," he said.

"Oh, she wouldn't!"

"Yes, she would."

"And he'd say to get rid of it."

"He'd do nothing of the sort. He's smarter than you are, or maybe even than I am."

"Could that possibly be?"

He stepped to her, picked her up, and sat down in the chair, holding her in his arms.

"You'll muss my uniform," she assured him.

"Tell the Supe you had an obstreperous patient." And he kissed her.

"How is Stowe smarter . . . ?" she asked, smoothing her hair.

"He knows children bind parents together."

"Oh, that." She smiled at him.

"It may take us nine or ten . . ."

"It may. Why did you break out in a rash, Tucker?"

"Because I saw you kissing your brother-in-law."

She sat straight up. "I never did!"

He pulled her down again into his embrace. "Don't contradict your next husband," he instructed her.

She gazed up into his face. "I don't really feel like laughing," she told him. "You look terrible too."

"I did see you kiss Stowe. Why shouldn't I look terrible?"

"Tuck . . ." she began, then she held his face between her hands. "Tuck, darling," she said softly, "have you done any crying about Bob?"

He pulled his face free. "Men can't cry," he said gruffly.

"Yes, they can. They do. Inside. That's why they break out in blisters."

"I saw you kissing Stowe Vashon," he insisted. "The man goes around bragging that he's in love with you."

"I don't believe that."

"Carrie . . ."

"You are Chief of Staff," she agreed, "but not when I am sitting on your lap."

"But he does . . ."

"He used to say he loved me. That was when I was fourteen. He says it since only to plague Megan. He —"

"Megan understands him. But I'll never understand her. And you did . . . kiss him!"

She sat thoughtful. Then her face brightened. "Yes, I did!" she agreed. "I remember. It was the night before Bob . . . Stowe kept lurking in corners, afraid to talk to you doctors. I was sorry for the man. It seemed that he just had nothing."

"We didn't any of us expect Bob to die."

"Of course we didn't. But surgery scares people. Megan had taken over. Stowe was in absolute torture. Fear, and anger . . ."

"So you kissed him."

"Yes, and I told him that everything would be all right. That you would take care of Bob."

"Oh, Carrie, you didn't!"

"I know I shouldn't have. But I did."

"And you kissed him. I wish you would feel sorry for me sometime."

She leaned back and studied his face. "I could never in the world be sorry for you, Tuck."

"Why not?"

She laid her cheek against his. "You haven't shaved in a week," she told him. "But I will kiss you."

She did, too. She kissed his cheek, she kissed his lips. And when she put her fingers to his cheeks she found them wet. "Oh, Tuck, Tuck," she said sorrowfully.

"I loved that kid," he said gruffly.

"I know you did. It —"

For a long minute they clung to one another. "That was a good kiss," he told her finally. To break his embarrassment.

"Better than the last time?" she asked.

"I don't remember the last time."

"Why, Tuck . . ."

"Because everything begins now," he explained to her. "What happened to your cap?"

"It's around somewhere. But —"

Their heads turned. The door was opening, and in it stood Dr. Moore, a short hospital robe over his even shorter hospital gown, terry cloth scuffs on his feet.

"What in hell are you doing out of bed?" Tuck roared at him.

"Well, everybody went off and left me. And I was pretty sure you'd need warning that you were about to get that rash again. And I have a schedule for the rest of this week . . ."

Carrie was attempting to get to her feet, straighten her uniform, and to find her cap, which was under Tuck's desk.

"If he does get it," she gasped, "the rash, I mean, it can't be infectious. And I'll take you back to bed."

"I got here on my own."

"And nobody stopped you? This is a great

hospital. Come along now."

Tuck stood up. "Any taking this guy to bed, I'll do it," he announced.

"The fellow's jealous," Dr. Moore told Carrie in surprise.

"Well, I certainly hope so. And do you know? He thinks kissing isn't normal."

"I'll make out a report on *that!*" Dr. Moore left the office and they heard some nurse asking him loudly what on earth he thought he was doing.

Tuck closed the office door. He gathered Carrie into his arms. "Kissing may not be normal," he told her, "but it is real nice."

"Yes, it is," she agreed. "Now, doctor, about that schedule of yours . . ."

He rummaged among the papers on his desk. "Let's get married," he said.

"We are going to."

"I can't find it on my schedule."

"Did you expect to?"

"Well, sure I did. It should head the list."

"But we are going to do it, and it won't need any hospital schedule . . ."

"I mean right now."

"*Now?*" she asked. "Me in a rumpled uniform, and you —"

"I mean right *now!* Why shouldn't we?"

"Well, I'd thought about flowers, and —"

"We can find flowers in any patient's

room, and we . . . Oh, damn," he said softly. For his pocket beeper was sounding. "Oh, gee . . ." he began, then broke off. He shook his head. "I can't say it," he told her solemnly.

She reached up and kissed him. "You will be able to, after a time," she said softly. "Aren't you needed in surgery?"

"I'll take you along. And then, this evening . . ."

"Did you ever find that schedule?"

"I wouldn't think of hunting for it."

She smiled at him. "This evening," she agreed. "As an emergency."

"It sure is one. Are you coming?"

"As soon as I put on my cap."

"Then I'll be seeing you." He strode out of the room, and she stood at the door, watching him walk down the hall. Triumph in every line of his tall, strong body.

"I am glad to see him back at work," said Mrs. Adams at her shoulder. "He took Bob's death very hard."

"He takes every death hard," said Carrie softly. "But he knows there will be other Bobs. That's why he is a doctor."

We hope you have enjoyed this Large Print book. Other Thorndike Press or Chivers Press Large Print books are available at your library or directly from the publishers.

For more information about current and upcoming titles, please call or write, without obligation, to:

Thorndike Press
P.O. Box 159
Thorndike, Maine 04986 USA
Tel. (800) 257-5157

OR

Chivers Press Limited
Windsor Bridge Road
Bath BA2 3AX
England
Tel. (0225) 335336

All our Large Print titles are designed for easy reading, and all our books are made to last.